THE RISING

THE CROOKED TALES SERIES

In reading order:
The Rising
Night of the Witch
(*Coming: October* 2024)

THE RISING

CROOKED TALES
BOOK ONE

CHRIS HARRISON

WICKED INK
PUBLISHING

This is a work of fiction, and the views expressed herein are the sole responsibility of the author. Likewise, characters, places, and incidents are the product of the author's imagination, and any resemblance to actual persons, living or dead, or actual events or locations, is entirely coincidental.

The Rising (Crooked Tales Series) : Book 1
Copyright © 2024 by Chris Harrison

Published by Wicked Ink Publishing Ltd.
www.wickedinkpublishing.com

Cover and book design © 2024 by Wicked Ink Publishing Ltd.
Editors: Raymond Griffiths & Adam Bamford

All rights reserved. No part of this book may be scanned, uploaded, reproduced, distributed, or transmitted in any form or by any means whatsoever without prior written permission from the publisher.

First Edition: June 2024
Printed in Canada

The National Library of Canada Cataloging -in-Publication Data is available upon request.

ISBN 978-1-998278-00-8 (paperback)
ISBN 978-1-998278-01-5 (ebook)

For Harry & Nikki

Secrets always dwell in the darkest shadows...

THE RISING

PROLOGUE

Thomas Rowe buckled under the weight of grief and sunk into the marshy grass beneath him. His crimson hands glistened under the moon's mournful gaze as he wrestled with the bludgeoning reality that had finally brought him to his knees. His love was gone. Someone violently took Jane, a god-fearing, kind, and remarkable woman whom he had loved for twenty years. Snatched by a horse-thief's murderous hands in a moment of panic.

What kind of God did this to his children?

It made no sense. Nothing did now. He tightened his eyelids, scrambling to reset his memory and unsee the images that had just been etched inside his mind.

The delicate trickle of blood escaping Jane's mouth as she lay staring beyond the starlit sky. Her innocent blood, warm on his rugged palms, beseeching him for justice as he thrust the knife into the cowering thief crying beside her.

Why her? Why now?

Thomas had built this home for her. Their haven in the woods, safe from the cursed lawless streets of Cold Christmas.

The heavens joined him in his sorrow as rain snaked its way down his balding head, flooding the jagged trenches of his weather-beaten skin. Watching the bloody waterfall cascade from his hands, tainting the soil that once offered so much hope and promise. A rage swelled within his throat; one he could no longer swallow or stomach.

"What use are your tears now?!" he rebuked.

His words tensed and flexed in the air like a genie escaping its dusty brass prison. The surrounding trees paid their respects, bowing to his all-consuming sadness, and rattling in fear of his indignation. He felt a storm stir inside him; a vicious whirlwind of bitterness and fury, devouring everything in its path until Thomas Rowe, the husband, the Christian, the man, was no more.

"I hate you!" he yelled at the onslaught of wind and rain, his voice echoing through the woods that surrounded him.

As the moon surrendered its light, darkness gently cradled the broken, blood-soaked man, inviting him to take refuge in the shadows.

An icy hand clasped the back of his neck, sending a sharp chill down to his tailbone.

"We've been waiting for you..." it whispered seductively.

The howling winds swallowed Thomas Rowe's final screams as the desolate sky wept for the fate of the world.

1

Creeeeeaaak!

Helen jolted and jumped up in bed with a start, unsure if the loose floorboard outside her room, or the remnants of her recurring nightmares, had woken her. Bleary-eyed, she glanced at the gap beneath her bedroom door just in time to catch the tail-end of a shadow drift by. Someone was inside the house!

"Jonath..." She turned over to wake her husband, only to painfully remind herself she was very much alone. The other half of the king-sized bed, where Jonathan had once laid curled beside her, was now barren and cold to the touch.

Creak!

The intruder returned to her door, lingering this time, and sealing the room in darkness. Helen's heart laboured at the realization there was a very real stranger prowling her house at night, as she fumbled to wake her phone. With a solitary click of her French manicured nail, its hazy glow painted the surrounding walls a dim dusty blue as she fought to adjust to the light.

Squeeeeeaaak!

Tucking a lock of thick black hair behind her ear, she squinted through the gloom and watched in horror as the door handle slowly turned. Someone on the other side wanted in.

She knew it couldn't be an old guest; it had been almost a week now since she'd closed the B&B's doors to the public, and all keys were accounted for. Scrolling through her contacts, she found DI Richards' number and quickly hit the call button.

Clatter!

Clatter!

Her bedroom door rattled violently in its frame, triggering a cold sweat as she waited for her call to connect. The room lock was a weak metal latch, unlikely to deter the trespasser for long.

"Hello?! Police please!" She bluffed, hoping it would deter her assailant. The rattling abruptly stopped just as DI Richards picked up.

"Mrs Ashfield? Is everything ok?" His tone was a little flippant, but he sounded alert given it was well after midnight.

"Someone is in the house," She whispered. "...an intruder. Please, send someone. They're trying to force their way into my room!" Helen glanced back at her door and could still see the uninvited shadow loitering at its base.

"I've called the police!" She shouted indignantly. "They're on their way!"

"Just stay put, Mrs Ashfield. I've got a car nearby, and it's on its way. Is there anything you can use to block the door until they arrive?"

The shadow remained defiant as Helen scanned the room for something to buy her some more time. The only item that wasn't bolted to the wall was a rustic chest of drawers at the foot of her bed, but now looking down the barrel of sixty, the likelihood of her being able to lug anything that heavy across the carpet on her own was pretty low.

Before she'd lost so much weight with worry, Helen would have required someone to talk her down from going out there to confront whoever it was, but seven stressful years had taken their toll and she now felt old for her age; bordering on frail.

Clatter!
Clatter!
Thud!

The door rattled once more before being dealt a heavy blow in anger. For a moment Helen thought it might break, but the wood and lock both held firm as the shadow slowly departed, drifting away silently into the night just as mysteriously as it had arrived.

"I think they've gone." She whispered to DI Richards. "I'm going to check."

As she forced herself to climb out of bed, she felt a sudden, sharp chill to her chest that took her breath away. Her pyjama top was drenched in sweat, as it often was these days.

For months now, strange thumping sounds at night had been plaguing her, always coming from the ground floor below and always around the same time.

She'd learned to live with it, as she had many other unusual things that occurred in that house, but tonight was different; tonight someone real had been at her door. Fraught with worry, she edged her way closer towards the door.

Creak!

Helen's heart leapt into her mouth as she found the only creaky floorboard in her room and froze in fear.

Watching the faint ray of light seeping into the carpet at her feet, she could hear the distant monotony of DI Richards telling her not to do anything stupid, but it was too late for that. Inches from the door, she pressed her head against the cold wooden panel to listen.

WOOP! WOOP!

Helen's entire body jerked as a siren echoed in the woods outside, filling her room with its swirling bright blue light.

"It's ok...they're here now." She muttered pensively, as she reached for the lock with a trembling hand and turned the key.

Click!

"Th...thank you Jason..." Helen trailed off as she opened her door, then rummaged to find the light switch for the neighbouring room. Its low-hanging bulb was dazzling at first as she struggled to adjust to the vivid white walls of the converted upstairs living space. The plush beige carpet felt soft and comforting beneath her feet as Helen ventured beyond the safety of her bedroom only to come to a sudden halt, dropping her phone on the floor in shock.

There on the wall right in front of her, scrawled in bright red dripping paint, were the words...

'GET OUT!'

2

"*...Well, that was local blues legend Ray Stone, belting out another classic from his latest album 'Heart of Stone'. Be sure to stop by and check him out this weekend when he headlines our Herts FM blues festival at the Hatfield Theatre. Tickets are available on hertsfm.co.uk/tickets and we've got quite the show for you all. We're hoping storm Seamus doesn't cause too much chaos when it strikes tonight, and you all come see us. So, on that note, we're now going to get the latest weather and travel in the area from Cindy. Cindy, over to you...*"

When DI Richards stopped by the next morning, he interrupted Helen scrubbing the paint from her living room wall while listening to her favourite radio station. Helen had just about enough of the Hertford police department as the two young police constables who had responded to her call made her feel like the village crackpot.

"So, I guess that's it now then, is it?!" she fumed as he entered the front porch. "I'm now the village kook, wasting valuable police time with my overactive imagination and paranoia. There was someone here last night, I swear it.

They almost broke my bedroom door down, for Christ's sake! But because your colleagues…who didn't look a day over fifteen I might add…because they couldn't find any sign of forced entry, I'm making it all up!"

Helen came from a long line of strong independent Greek women, and she could feel her fiery temper getting the better of her as she remonstrated with the rather meek looking detective standing in her entrance hall.

"Nobody thinks that at all, Mrs Ashfield, I assure you. We all know what you've been through…what you're still going through." DI Richards had all the hallmarks of a pen-pusher in Helen's eyes.

His entire demeanour was one of compliance; a yes man, always on hand to tell her exactly what she wanted to hear to pacify her. Anything for an easy life, she thought as she clocked him surreptitiously surveying the pile of cardboard boxes over her shoulder.

In his early forties, DI Richards was as average as they come; standing only a few inches taller than her, he had cropped thinning brown hair on top of his weaselly face, and a paunch that told her he spent more time sitting at his desk than he did chasing criminals.

"Well, you won't have to worry about me for much longer. I'm packing my bags and going." She barked, before turning around and marching back upstairs. "Well, come on then, don't just stand there gawping. Come and look at the latest figment of my imagination!"

DI Richards folded his khaki quilted jacket over his arm and skulked up the stairs behind her.

"There! See? Why would I tell myself to '*get out*' when I'm already going? What possible reason would I have to do this? And why ruin my lovely carpet?" Helen scoffed, pointing at the washed-out threat plastered across her wall and deep red stain that had soaked into the carpet beneath it.

DI Richards studied the graffiti for a moment and stroked his greying stubble.

"Nobody's saying we don't believe you Mrs Ashfield, it's just that this is the fifth time you've called my office now to report a disturbance, and whenever I've sent someone out here, they've always come back empty-handed. We can only go by what we see, I'm afraid, and based on the report I found on my desk this morning, last night gave us nothing. Now we both know the reputation this place has; from what I can gather, that's why you and your husband bought it all those years ago. As I've said before, old houses often make strange noises from time to time. A woman living here on her own, cut off from the rest of the village...no guests to keep you busy or keep you company...I'm pretty sure I'd be freaked out too as soon as the sun went down."

"You sound just like the two kids you sent here last night!" Helen rolled her eyes as she plunged the sponge back into the soapy bucket of water. "You know, there is more to this place than idle gossip and creaky floorboards. Why don't you ask your dad why he and your mum used to stay here every year? Or why half your police force gets twitchy the moment they're asked to step foot near the place? I know what I saw last night. Someone else was here. I wasn't imagining things, and this time it wasn't a bloody ghost."

Creak!

Helen flinched as DI Richards stepped on the same loose floorboard the intruder had.

"See!" she snapped. "Whoever it was, stood right there." Helen knelt down to continue scrubbing as DI Richards inched his way back towards the staircase.

"Where will you go?" He probed, slipping back into his jacket.

"I haven't decided yet, but one thing's for sure: it'll be far away from this god forsaken place! Seven years Jason. Seven years I've searched...and nothing. Not one lead on where Jonathan went that night. And now here I am, on the brink of being declared a widow with absolutely nothing to show for it. I have sunk every penny I had into finding him. I've sunk it all into keeping this bloody place going, hoping that one day he'd come back to me." Helen's eyes welled up as she directed all her anger at the wall in front of her, scouring at the smeared pink stain.

"This was his dream, Jason, his dream! He loved it here, and we were happy, until...until it all became too much. I lost him to this bloody place. Whatever happened...this place had something to do with it, I know it! I just can't prove it. So now it's time for me to walk away. I can't stay anymore..." Helen rang the sponge out and slumped next to the bucket in defeat.

"I'm truly sorry, Mrs Ashfield, for everything. Is there anyone you can stay with until your move date? Any family, or a friend, perhaps?"

"The sooner I close everything down here, the sooner I can be on my way. Then it can rot for all I care. Let the ghosts have it. No good will ever come of this place..."

Helen cuffed her tears and got back to her feet in defiance. "But until then, I'm not letting anyone run me out of my home. When I go, it'll be on my terms!"

"I understand." DI Richards gave a sombre nod and retreated downstairs. "I'll keep an ear to the ground in case anything turns up. Maybe see if I can get a patrol to drive by here later as a precaution...There's a storm coming tonight and we're expecting it to be a doozy. In the meantime, though, you know how to reach me if you need anything. Take care Helen, please. I'll let myself out."

And in his usual fashion, DI Richards slunk away back to the safety of his desk, delivering nothing of any consequence.

3

It was a little after 4pm by the time Helen had finally removed all trace of the threatening message, and the sun had already started its descent. Pinching her shoulder blades together, she tried to trap the ice-cold shiver that was scuttling its way up her spine at the prospect of spending another night alone.

Then it dawned on her.

If she was to stand any chance of getting some sleep that night, she'd need to make sure the guest rooms were all secure. Even though she considered him useless, she should have done it when DI Richards stopped by, but at the time she had been too preoccupied with her own outrage. She faced the daunting task of checking every door and window, room by room, alone. Although the patronizing PC Phillips had assured her he'd checked them all last night, her confidence levels in the police were at an all-time low, so she needed to see for herself.

As Helen crept downstairs and met the cooler air, she felt another shudder brewing in the small of her back, so she wrapped her grey woollen cardigan around her and fastened her tie-belt to stifle it.

Since closing the B&B to the public, she had switched the heating off in the lower level to save money, and the moment she entered the communal living space it felt as if she'd stepped into a giant refrigerator. A stale, musty smell had already coalesced in the absence of any guests, and the kitchen service bar was collecting dust. The building itself resembled a cube, with a modest kitchen-diner at its heart, framed by ten guest rooms, a tiny office, and a small library for guests who wanted to brush up on the creepy history of the area.

Renowned for being haunted, Jonathan had put a great deal of time and effort into making sure no guest ever walked away disappointed, although as time went on the ghosts had needed less and less encouragement to make their presence felt. Every single person who stayed there left with some kind of spooky story to tell their friends about, and as their reputation grew, Jonathan became more and more obsessed with the history of the place.

Towards the end, Helen watched that obsession drive a firm wedge between them as he spent more and more time in the office at night, filling his head with a wild assortment of urban legends, until one night he never left.

DI Richards was a PC back then, but he'd insisted Jonathan had left her, perhaps to start afresh somewhere else, but Helen always knew this house had something to do with it. Despite the number of years that had passed, and the handful of private investigators she'd hired to find him, nothing had ever yielded so much as a clue, let alone any answers.

Jonathan Ashfield had vanished without a trace.

"C'mon Helen, let's get this over with." She muttered.

Deciding to start in the library, her plan was to work her way around all the rooms in reverse order as quickly as possible, then head back upstairs and lock herself in her room. In all her time there, it was only ever the guest rooms that seemed to attract the attention of spirits, so the library would serve as a relatively safe reintroduction to the house, unless, of course, the intruder had returned.

Helen's blood pressure rose, and she came over a little queasy at the prospect of finding someone waiting for her on the other side of the door. A hundred what ifs muddied her mind, each one tainted by the countless gruesome tales of murder she'd heard Jonathan rattle off to unsuspecting guests.

Taking a deep breath to steady her nerves, she listened intently. The house fell into an eerie silence, making Helen ponder if it was the calm before the storm.

The library door let out a soft *creak* as she opened it to step inside, and she was relieved to see both window latches tightly fastened above the old pine desk.

Glancing at the bookshelves, Helen was transported to happier times, when she and Jonathan were just starting out as landlords; visiting various markets and car-boot sales to pick up spooky accessories to help decorate the place and ramp up the atmosphere. They were both so excited to have a project they could dive into together, having taken the plunge to leave their boring office jobs behind them.

She felt a lump rise to her throat as she remembered their first night there; the entire house to themselves, creeping around with torches like amateur sleuths trying to wake the dead. She wished she could go back in time to that day; warn her younger self of the nightmare that lay in wait. *How could so much tragedy and horror befall one house?*

She knew the answer, of course; it was the house itself. She felt its evil even now, simmering beneath the surface, waiting patiently for night to fall.

Click!

She closed the door on her bittersweet trip down memory lane and wandered past the storage cupboard onto room 10. This one had the least activity of all ten rooms and as Helen opened its door and poked her head inside, it only just then dawned on her that there was a pattern to the place.

The higher the room number, the fewer paranormal encounters seemed to occur, although by the time Jonathan had finished with each guest, it didn't matter where they stayed; they'd be sure to experience something unsettling, be that a ghost or their own amped up imagination.

Each room mostly comprised the same rustic furniture along with the odd creepy ornament or picture thrown in for good measure here and there. Jonathan would often make up stories connecting each item to the house to help stir the pot, but the truth was, he rarely needed to.

Along with its free-standing oak wardrobe and antique bed, room 10's bonus item was a surreal oil painting they had found in a second-hand shop on the outskirts of town one sunny Saturday afternoon. It had more than a hint of Dali to it, depicting a young boy in a hood, devoid of any colour, solemnly crouched beneath a melting purple and amber tree scape. Jonathan had said it reminded him of the woods outside, and from a distance the trees in the painting looked like two giant hands, collapsing in on the dejected-looking boy. The artist was anonymous but etched in the canvas corner was the title '*Reckoning*'.

Helen could almost hear Jonathan stringing guests along with his story of how the artist had been a local talent who'd gone insane, painting the same scene repeatedly before taking his own life one night in the woods. He was such a talented storyteller, and in his element when taking guests on a tour of the property. Satisfied the room was secure, Helen closed the door and moved on.

"Huh!" Helen jumped right out of her skin the second she entered room 9. She'd forgotten about the large mirror facing the door and hadn't expected her reflection to greet her. "Silly cow!" she snapped, cross with herself, before adding glumly. "God, you look old Helen!"

There was a strange metallic odour in the room that wafted over her as she ventured inside, but she had no intention of investigating it.

Shaking off her initial jitters, she scampered over to the window and pulled the curtain back a little so she could see the latch. "All locked." She declared and then gazed up at the sky outside. The clouds were rolling in quickly now, suffocating what little was left of the evening sun.

She had to get a move on, as the last place she wanted to be was downstairs alone when it got dark.

THUD!

As she closed the door, she heard a muffled sound from the next room that made her blood run cold.

Room 7 was the latest to 'play up' as she called it, and the last few guests to stay there had all complained of being woken in the night by someone crashing about in their room. Despite receiving multiple complaints, she never found any signs of movement or damage when inspecting the room, and although she had never personally witnessed anything unusual in there, she had been hearing the same noises every night like clockwork.

CRACK!

Helen flinched as the second noise rang out, breaking

the unnatural silence within the house like a heavy branch being snapped in two. Usually upstairs when it occurred. This was the closest she'd been to the source of the commotion.

Someone or something had to be in there.

4

Rooted to the spot, Helen waited in the hallway, listening out for another noise to come from room 7, but nothing did.

The sequence was always the same; a dull *thud* followed by a sharp *crack*.

Although she could feel her heart thumping ten-to-the-dozen in her ears, she couldn't bear calling DI Richards twice in as many days based on a couple of strange noises.

Up close, the last noise, however, had been beyond strange and sounded almost violent in its nature; final.

She tried to rationalize it, explain it away as a tree knocking against the window in the wind, but there wasn't a tree close enough on that side of the house. Of course, as DI Richards mansplained to her, most old buildings creaked from time to time, but hers was not like most other buildings.

Dry-mouthed, Helen plucked up the courage to move, tiptoeing towards the door to room 7 and placing an ear to it.

Nothing.

The only sound she could hear was her own throat, labouring in desperate pursuit of saliva.

"C'mon Hels," She whispered, reaching out for the door handle.

"Ow!" She retracted her hand immediately. The brass handle was so cold it stung to the touch, like grabbing a frozen snowball with bare hands. Pulling the sleeve of her cardigan down for protection, she tried again.

Click!

The door gave her the slip, swinging open of its own accord with a loud creak and Helen winced; bracing herself for whatever might be waiting for her inside, but from where she stood, the room looked empty.

In the western corner of the house, she had a pretty good vantage point from the doorway, but there was one window latch annoyingly tucked around the corner, next to the ensuite, which remained just out of sight. A dusky haze filled the room, tainting everything it touched with gloomy shades of brown and grey. The clock was ticking, so Helen forced herself to enter, creeping across the natural stone floor tiles until the window came into view.

Once inside the room, it felt bitterly cold, as if she was standing outside in the middle of the woods on a cold winter night. With each breath she took, a tiny cloud of vapour hung momentarily in the stale stuffy air, only to dissolve just in time for the next cloud to take its place.

Aside from her own heavy breathing, room 7 was perfectly still.

The bed remained made and untouched since the last time she had been in there, the wardrobe was closed, and there was no other sign of a disturbance until.

"What th..." Her shoulders slumped as the tension she'd been carrying swiftly gave way to bewilderment.

On top of the small oak chest of drawers, beneath the window she couldn't quite see from the doorway, was another of Jonathan's spooky conversation pieces; this time one she absolutely loathed.

"What are you doing in here?" She wondered aloud, ambling over to the macabre sculpture.

Tipped onto its side was a cast iron bust; its coarsely crafted, androgynous face was the epitome of suffering. Eyes closed and twisted in torment; a disturbing veil of faux barbed wire caged the grim-looking statuette.

Helen hated it.

Jonathan, however, loved it, having found the piece at a local auction whilst on the hunt for furniture. Of all the items he'd come back with, this was the one that required no make-believe backstory or introduction to make an impression; it was terrifying.

But that wasn't Helen's problem with it today.

Her problem was, someone had moved it from its rightful place in the dreaded room 4, and that someone most definitely hadn't been her. The item itself weighed a ton, and she remembered Jonathan sweating and straining when he carted it in from the car that day. 'How scary is this?' he'd gushed, unboxing it in front of her.

Of course, they didn't know back then just how at home it would be in room 4. There was a lot they didn't know about this place back then. What had started out as a fun, gimmicky, business opportunity had descended into a sinister attack on her sanity, robbing her of everything she held dear.

Helen shivered at the prospect of checking the remaining rooms and promised herself this would be the last night she ever spent there.

5

With renewed impetus from her unsettling encounter in room 7, Helen made light work of checking rooms 6 to 5, even ensuring the back door to the building was secure in between.

Fortunately, Helen saw most of the windows on that side of the house clearly from the safety of the door, so she didn't even need to venture in.

Room 4, however, was a different story with its corner plot and awkward layout. It required her to enter inside a little if she wanted to be sure. Of all the rooms, that was the one she avoided at all costs. No matter what time of day she went in there, she never felt safe.

When Jonathan was around, he'd always made up that room for any incoming guests and taken care of its general upkeep when empty. Thinking about it now, Helen realized she hadn't stepped foot in there for almost seven years, having closed it to the public the moment she'd been left to fend for herself, but there was no ducking out of it now.

Her imagination went into overdrive as she limbered up to its door, remembering the last time she had gone in there.

It had all been building up to that point.

Each time she made up the room, she would feel somebody's eyes on her, burning a hole in her back as she made the bed and dusted the furniture. It was way beyond being watched though, it was as if she was being stalked.

Of course, she'd heard all the stories; guests complaining about a sinister figure standing over them at night, watching them from the shadows.

For a while she wondered if it was just a stunt Jonathan had pulled to keep the place relevant, but after a while she felt it too; a presence so unsettling it made her flesh creep, until one day, while bending down to clean the skirting, she felt its breath on the back of her neck.

Even the memory of it made her skin crawl; the moist feeling it left on her nape, the putrid smell of halitosis. But it was the reflection that had tipped her over the edge; she'd caught it on the tv as she jumped to her feet. It had been there for less than a second, ambiguous in the gloom of the flat screen, yet it had left an indelible mark on her spirit.

A shadowy mountain of a man, brawny arms poised, waiting to grab her, and then it was gone.

She never went in there again after that.

Knowing her luck, of all the rooms to be harbouring an intruder, this would be the one most likely.

"Better get it over with, I suppose..." She mumbled to herself, white-knuckled, gripping the door handle.

Taking a deep breath, Helen slowly pushed the door ajar and peeked in through the gap.

A fleeting waft of petrol clung to the roof of her mouth, and then evaporated as a tornado of dust particles twirled beneath the fading daylight, then corkscrewed their way to the centre of the room as she opened the door wider.

The room was exactly as she'd remembered, only caked

in a thick layer of grime that looked more like ash from a fire.

Helen stepped onto the red rug in the room's centre and saw that the window was still fastened, which made her breathe a sigh of relief.

Surveying the rest of the room, her eyes were drawn to the perfectly preserved circle of dark mahogany on the chest of drawers where the bust had once stood, and it confirmed someone had been in there recently. She wondered if it was the same person hellbent on driving her out and decided she'd seen enough.

Click!

She locked the door from the outside and took a moment to gather herself. There was no doubt in her mind now; she had to leave. As soon as tonight's storm had passed, she would pack her bag and go.

6

THE REST OF THE ROOMS WERE EASY TO INSPECT compared to room 4, and when Helen made it back upstairs, it was close to 5pm. The kitchen radio had been playing to itself since she'd finished cleaning the wall and so she lingered a while to catch the local news.

"...well, officials have now increased the local weather warning from amber to red. That means people are being advised to stay home and avoid traveling unless it's an absolute emergency. Winds of up to 48 kilometres per hour are expected to hit from around midnight, along with several inches of rain. Here's the latest update from our eye in the sky. Cindy, over to you..."

Click!

Helen switched the radio off and put the kettle on.

If it wasn't for the increased weather warning, she might have gone tonight. She'd kept enough money back to put her up somewhere until Jonathan's insurance paid out, and then she could put this place firmly in her rear-view mirror. A removal company could collect the rest of her things once she was settled. She'd already given the access codes to

Jonathan's friend Peter, which meant they would have someone to let them in, and she would need never return.

"I'm sorry Jon." She sighed over the lump in her throat at the prospect of giving up. "I've done everything I can, but now it's time to face reality; you're gone and you're not coming back."

Buzz...

Helen flinched as the radio came back to life behind her, booming out a creepy concoction of white noise and static.

"Grr! This fucking place!" She fumed, marching over to switch it off again. Unplugging it from the wall this time, the whistling wind instantly replaced its eerie melody outside.

Seamus was coming.

7

By 9pm that evening, the storm was in full swing, lashing the windows with rain and rattling the woodland outside.

After her dry microwave lasagne for one, Helen had spent most of the evening in floods of tears as she packed her bag for the morning. She couldn't believe it had come to this. A house full of promise, now haunted by ghosts; some too painful to bear.

Dabbing her eyes with the cuff of her cardigan, she fetched a glass of water and returned to her bedroom, this time locking the door behind her.

Room by room, she had said her goodbyes, and now, both physically and emotionally exhausted, all she wanted to do was rest her bloodshot eyes and go to sleep. As she closed the curtains, she heard the gravel outside and watched as a police car pulled up.

Doing a laboured three-point turn in the carpark, it floodlit the dense wall of trees that surrounded the house before disappearing again into the darkness.

At least DI Richards had delivered on one of his

promises, she thought, and then continued shutting herself off from the outside world.

The moment Helen climbed into bed, she felt the day's tension dissipate beneath the cool, cotton bedsheets. Doubling up her pillow, she did all she could to get comfortable and then closed her eyes.

Outside, the storm had eased up a little, leaving the wind to dance amongst the trees; whistling and rustling up the perfect lullaby just for her, and within a matter of minutes, Helen was sound asleep.

Thud!

CRACK!

The same disturbing sequence of noises that had been haunting her yanked her from her slumber, Helen sat bolt upright with a start.

BOOM!

A rejuvenated Seamus was raging once more, and her room had been plunged into total darkness.

The roll of thunder rumbled beyond the woods outside, and she guessed the storm had caused a blackout. Bracing herself for the lightning that was sure to follow, she rubbed the vestiges of sleep from her eyes and anxiously waited.

"One Mississippi. Two Mississippi. Three Mississippi... Aaaah!"

Lightning filled the room with a vibrant flash of electricity and Helen screamed in horror.

At the foot of her bed, atop the chest of drawers, sat the ghoulish iron bust from downstairs. It stared at her ominously through closed eyes as the light struck its soulless face, and then, in an instant, it was gone again as Helen was cast back once more into blackness.

In a frenzy, she groped for her phone in the dark whilst

wrestling to temper the adrenaline coursing through her bloodstream.

BOOM!

The thunder roared again, closer this time, as it rattled her windows and shattered what was left of her nerves.

Helen felt her breath desert her as she spiralled close to hyperventilating, and then the lightning struck once more.

The one-two punch of pure terror shook her to her core, as the gruesome sculpture reared its hideous face again, corrupting her room with its thorny shadow, before vanishing beneath the cover of darkness.

Helen found the flashlight on her phone and shone it at the door.

"B...but how!" She stuttered, as the head of a brass chub key glinted back at her from within its lock, just the way she'd left it.

BOOM!

Another clap bellowed out from above, and the iron abomination toppled onto its side. Lightning followed, and there, tangled within the barbed wire, she saw Jonathan's face; eyes wide and screaming in sheer fright.

She took aim with her flashlight only to find the face had returned to its familiar, genderless guise.

Was DI Richards and his cronies right? Had she lost her mind?

Whatever the answer, she couldn't stay here.

With the power out, Helen realized she wouldn't have phone service to call for help.

So, she hauled herself out from under the covers and was greeted by an icy chill, similar to what she felt downstairs. Standing now, shivering in the bitter air, she retrieved her cardigan from the floor and hastily wrapped it around her. She'd only made it a couple of steps toward the door before fear took hold and Helen came to a grinding halt in the middle of the room.

What if the intruder was still inside the house, hiding somewhere amongst the shadows?

BOOM!

The heavens' latest roar jolted her out of her daze with a start. She darted to the window and peered outside just as the lightning struck.

"Noooo!" She cried, as the sudden burst of light exposed a sinister hooded figure lurking at the edge of the woods, creeping towards the house.

Helen raced to her door, cursing and floundering as she tried to turn the key and get out.

Click!

Flashlight in hand, she bundled her way into the living room.

She had to get downstairs.

The circuit breaker was at the rear of the house, on a wall between rooms 6 and 8. Once she had power, she could lock herself in a room and wait for the keystone cops to arrive.

Buzzzzzzz!

The radio came to life from the opposite corner, filling the air with crackly white noise.

Head spinning, Helen flashed at the source, tracing the power cable with her light only to find the plug laying pins-up on the worktop.

"*Get out... get out... get out...*" A discord of ghostly whispering voices danced along the airwaves and chased her down the stairs.

BOOM!

Helen's legs turned to jelly as the thunder echoed up the staircase, sending her toppling down its remaining steps.

Sprawled on her hands and knees inside the porch, she looked up at the glass door as lightning rained down once again.

"AAAAAH!" Her shrill scream was swallowed by the howling wind outside as she came face to face with her assailant.

Hands pressed against the glass; his hooded silhouette cast an ominous shadow over her trembling body as she scrambled to get back to her feet on the slippery stone floor. Racing through the downstairs living room and past the kitchen-diner Helen heard the impish, high-pitched giggling of a small child echo behind her as she turned the last corner into the hallway.

It was as if the storm had woken every malevolent spirit in the house and they were now conspiring to drive her out.

Dizzy with fear, Helen clattered into the wall as she turned to check behind her, but the murky corridor was empty.

BOOM!

The door to room 4 burst wide open just as the latest roll of thunder struck.

For a split second, under the flickering strobe of brilliant white light, a huge, hulking shadow of a man flashed across the floor and then vanished as quickly as it came.

Helen screamed again, reeling away from the menacing presence, and began frantically rattling door handles in search of somewhere to hide.

CRASH!

The sharp clinking of shattering glass clattered down the hall behind her; someone had broken through the back door!

Her head was pounding now, as every story, every

urban myth she'd ever overheard about the monster in room 4 came flooding back to her at once, drowning her in fear.

One by one by one, each door denied her sanctuary from whatever phantoms were now hunting her, until she came to room 7. Reaching out for its brass handle, she felt the static of the storm flow through her fingertips as the door swung open and the rampant winds gave way to deafening silence.

"Jonathan?!" She cried, overcome with confusion and disbelief.

8

Helen froze in shellshocked silence at the sight of her missing husband.

A sudden surge of power caused the bulb overhead to flicker and flare before settling on a soft amber glow as the edges of her vision softened and blurred like the vignette of a dream.

This couldn't be!

Inside room 7, Jonathan Ashfield stood before her, large as life, and not a day older than the last time she had seen him. His greying hair was dishevelled, and he appeared haggard; fraught with worry, just as he had been in the days leading up to that ill-fated evening.

"Jonathan..." She broke down, as years of grief caught up with her, sapping every ounce of what little energy she had left, but her husband didn't move a muscle. Instead, he stared straight through her; his tired brown eyes consumed with sadness. Beside him on the floor was a green plastic petrol can, its shiny black nozzle upright and ready to pour.

"Jonathan...what..." Helen took a shuffling step towards him, then paused, flummoxed and bewildered, as he continued to ignore her. His eyes came alive, as if he'd seen her, but his expression was one of scorn.

"YOU!" He shouted and charged towards her.

Helen flinched, closing her eyes in a state of utter disarray. In her blind recoil she felt a rush of air pass her by, carrying with it the familiar scent of Jonathan's cologne. How she'd missed that exquisite smell. She'd spent years spraying it around the house and on her pillow at night, but never downstairs.

THUD!

She recognized the noise immediately; its source now revealed as the clumsy sound of Jonathan falling snapped her out of her dreamy trance and she spun around to find him slumped on the floor in the room's corner.

Looming over him with his back to her was a monstrous giant of a man clutching the iron bust in one hand as if it were a hollow movie prop. Dressed in black, his skin looked deathly pale; dusty even, with thick white hair, spiked up on end atop his towering frame.

Cowering beneath him, Jonathan opened his mouth to scream, but all that escaped was a desperate gasp.

Before Helen had a chance to react and rush to his aid, he was callously snuffed out with a final ferocious swing of the monster's arm.

CRACK!

The vicious blow connected with Jonathan's temple, echoing around the room, snapping his neck to one side.

"AAAAAH!" Helen screamed; the sickening sound bringing her to her knees as it reverberated around the room.

Her husband's tormented face, still frozen in terror, lay rigidly on his shoulder at full tilt, while his white, lifeless eyes retreated within their sockets.

Helen couldn't move.

She couldn't speak.

It was as if she had been murdered, rather than the one forced to watch, as all the oxygen fled her lungs and left her hyperventilating on the floor.

In her shock-induced scramble for breath, the dreamy amber light faded around her, taking with it her dead husband's crumpled body and any trace of what had happened to him on that terrible night he went missing. All, that was, except Jonathan's murderer, who lingered in triumph, slowly turning to face her.

Still gasping for air, Helen trembled in the shadow of a brute who looked as if he'd been freshly carved from a block of marble. His colossal physique dominated the room as he starred at her with soulless eyes, black as night.

A sneer formed in the corner of his mouth, and then crept across the rest of his chiselled face as he menacingly stormed towards her.

BOOM!

The door to room 7 slammed shut, sealing her fate, as the rumbling of thunder swallowed Helen Ashfield's last desperate screams for mercy.

4 MONTHS LATER

9

Nancy's shadow impetuously raced ahead of her as she tiptoed along the dimly lit hallway.

A drop of blood glanced her shoulder, sneaking down her arm unnoticed before grinding to a halt in the thick wool of her cream cardigan, as she crept towards her brother's bedroom door. The next drop connected flush with her cheek, leaving a warm trail as it snaked its way towards her jawline.

Flinching, she stepped back and instinctively cuffed her face, gasping at the bright red smear staring back at her. Another drop landed on her open, outstretched palm and she fought desperately to swallow the scream clawing its way up towards her mouth.

Wiping her face, Nancy felt herself teeter on the brink of hysteria, but knew she had to look above her. She could see more droplets falling in front of her now, catching the light as they fell like a dripping tap of death.

Taking a slow, deliberate blink, she forced her eyes up toward the ceiling and stared at the pool of blood ominously expanding overhead.

A feeling of dread snatched her heart down into the pit of

her stomach as she imagined whose blood it might be. Her suspicions shattered any composure she had left to its core, and a muffled cry of desperation clambered its way out from between her pursed lips.

Nancy tightened her grip on the carving knife she had snatched from the kitchen. A floorboard, softly creaking behind her echoed the squeak of her clammy palm on the smooth wooden handle.

She spun around on the spot thrusting the knife out in front of her blindly, but there was no-one there.

'BANG!'

Her brother's door burst open and a bulky silhouette wearing a blood-soaked pantomime mask barged her to the ground.

Winded and frozen in shock, Nancy could only watch on in terror as the towering figure took a huge backswing with his axe.

Her final shrill scream punctured the air as the axe came down in Nancy's direction.

Fade to black...

"*As one door closes, another one shuts,*" thought Kane as he stared at his screen in defeat.

It was something his great uncle used to mutter to himself when things didn't go his way, and it had always stuck with him.

He briefly studied his murky reflection in the monitor.

Kane believed he had the right 'look' to be an online influencer with his on trend shaggy fringe and '*boy next door*' good looks. When he was younger, people had teased him for resembling an elf, but he'd matured now and grown into his features.

Kane pushed his thick, chocolate brown hair away from his face with both hands and rested his elbows on his desk in resignation. He had been posting videos every day without fail for over a month now and his followers had peaked at a measly five people. His gaze shifted to the number 5 in the hope it would suddenly increase...

Nothing.

One of the 5 was his younger brother, which made his progress even more pathetic.

Kane's latest offering was a reaction video to the new, and much hyped, slasher movie '*It's Behind You 6*'. He'd used some of his pocket money to rent the movie online and had done his absolute best to inject some excitement and humour to his reactions, but the bottom line was the movie sucked. In fact, it was an epic failure on so many levels, but big budget horror movies were few and far between.

This was all so much harder than he expected.

The dream of his *Scarytales* channel blowing up and quitting school early to live his best life looked to be nothing more than a pipe-dream now. In fact, if he was honest with himself, it had all become a chore lately. He needed inspiration, and an axe-wielding maniac wearing a creepy mask murdering dumb, predictable, pretty teenagers wasn't doing it.

"There's got to be something I can do..." Kane muttered to himself, "something new and exciting..."

Tap tap tap!

Kane froze as his fight-or-flight response fired up its engine and weighed up the sudden interruption.

"Are you recording?" whispered the tiny voice through Kane's bedroom door.

The handle turned presumptuously, and the door opened to reveal Zach standing there with a look of excitement etched across his freckled face.

Zach was Kane's biggest fan and younger brother. He

had a wiry frame and was substantially smaller than his idol, even when taking their three-year age gap into account. They shared the same features and haircut, so Zach was often referred to as '*mini-me*' by Kane's friends.

Kane was tall for fourteen, thanks to a growth spurt at the age of twelve. His parents bemoaned the regular shopping trips for clothes, but Kane loved being big for his age. He was often mistaken for being older and treated that way as a result. It was a perk he enjoyed using to his advantage, particularly at the local cinema.

Kane looked at his little brother grinning in the doorway and wondered if he would get the same growth spurt in a year or two. As he contemplated what that growth spurt might look like, Zach piped up again.

"I've just watched your latest post, and it was awesome! What's it like being famous?"

Even this well-timed bit of hero worshiping couldn't snap Kane out of the funk he was in about his embarrassing level of success. Zach had no concept of real success yet. He just saw his older brother online and immediately assumed he'd '*made it*', whatever that meant these days.

"Do you think mum and dad would let me watch that movie?" Zach asked.

"I doubt it spud," replied Kane. "Too much blood and guts for you! It'll give you nightmares."

Zach's excitement swiftly changed to disappointment, as if his body had suffered a power outage. His head and shoulders slumped beneath the weight of Kane's crushing rejection. Even his knees bent a little.

Zach often relied on dramatic reactions to gain sympathy and renegotiate. It wasn't an exact science, and occasionally it made things worse, but it was his go-to approach whenever he was told 'no'. It was just a 'phase' according to his parents, but Kane was more cynical and believed he'd been playing the sympathy card since birth.

Zach looked up beneath his brown wavy mop with feigned puppy dog eyes in the hope his older brother would reconsider.

"Maybe I could watch it in here...I won't tell mum and dad."

"I'm afraid I can't let you , so you can spare me the routine," Kane said, brushing his fringe out of his eyes. "I'm glad you liked my video, though."

"What will you do for your next one?" asked Zach. He had dropped his parody and was now scrutinizing the open laptop like a magpie.

Kane stared blankly through his brother, distracted, as he wondered if he should just pack the whole thing in.

"Now that's the million-dollar question," he said, half to himself.

It was a bright, brisk Saturday morning and Kane's best friend and co-conspirator, JJ, was due round any minute to brainstorm ideas for today's video. So far, Kane had nothing inspiring to offer, his obsession with all things horror only seemed to be shared by five people so far, including JJ and Zach. The thought was jarring as he looked back at the number five on his screen. It was more like three in reality, and those were all Zach's friends, so it felt more like a big fat zero.

Maybe it was time to quit, he wondered.

Ding dong!

Kane jumped again as the emphatic chime of the doorbell echoed up the stairs, abruptly interrupting his spiralling trance. Their dad suffered from poor hearing, so they had the volume set to max on most things in order to compensate. As a result, whenever anyone rang the doorbell, or the phone, it would often carry with it the threat of a cardiac arrest.

"It's ok, I've got it!" his dad called from downstairs.

James Jordan, or JJ, as he preferred to be called, was a couple of months younger than Kane and a few inches shorter. They'd known each other since kindergarten and had been inseparable ever since. JJ had light brown skin, hazel eyes, and an infectious smile which could light up the room.

He was just the tonic Kane needed right now.

JJ was the most positive and optimistic person Kane had ever met, but they both had a morbid fascination with horror movies; the scarier the better. They loved watching them together too; it was their Monday evening ritual after school. JJ was equally interested in the more technical aspects of filmmaking and loved his gadgets, which made them a perfect combination for *Scarytales*. They both shared lofty aspirations of making a career out of their online endeavours and renting an apartment in the city together, even moving to LA one day.

First, they had to break through the barrier of five followers.

"I've had a wicked idea," he announced as he entered Kane's room. "Fancy a donut?" JJ waved the box of jam donuts between Kane and Zach, who had now perched himself on the edge of his brother's bed to get the scoop on JJ's news.

"It's a bit early for donuts mate," Kane replied. "Besides, I've lost my appetite since I saw the viewing figures for yesterday's video."

JJ was grinning from ear to ear as he took another donut for himself and placed the box on Zach's lap. Being an only child, he treated Kane's younger brother as his own and often brought enough snacks for the three of them. He also had a soft spot for food, but despite his slightly bulkier frame, he was deceptively athletic. JJ tugged at the visor on his signature 'LA' baseball cap and then glided across Kane's bedroom towards the desk.

"Don't worry about that," he said, opening a new tab on Kane's browser. JJ's sugary hands dusted the keyboard as he typed 'Crooked House, Cold Christmas' before hitting the enter key triumphantly. He scrolled through the search results and selected the link titled 'Owner of haunted B&B reported missing'.

Boom!

JJ exclaimed before taking another huge bite of his donut. Kane and Zach looked on in wonder and then proceeded to frantically read the article.

Reclusive B&B owner feared missing after friends claim not to have seen or heard from her in over three months!

Helen Ashfield, 57, has been marred by tragedy since her husband Jonathan mysteriously vanished in 2015 (see the full story here). Despite an exhaustive search by local police, he was eventually declared dead in February 2022.

After funding a variety of private investigators to locate him, friends say Helen never gave up hope her husband would one day return. Unfortunately, he never did, and three months ago Helen was finally forced to close the doors of Crooked House to the public.

Since then, the deserted B&B, located on the outskirts of a tiny village named Cold Christmas, has become a regular haunt for local teens looking for scares. However, this isn't the boutique B&B's first brush with mystery.

Since its original owner brutally murdered his wife

and her lover, the historic building (built in the early 1700s) has had a link to witchcraft and the paranormal.

Rumour has it he was never caught and is now one of the many spirits said to wander the halls at night. Our sources say it is this ghostly appeal which first attracted Helen and Jonathan to buy the building in 2001 and provided them with a steady stream of guests on the hunt for ghosts.

Interest in Crooked House peaked twelve years ago when it was featured in the 2010 edition of 'Britain's Most Haunted Hotels' by famed author and historian Peter Higginsworth, so it's no surprise it's beginning to draw attention again now it has been abandoned.

Detective Inspector Richards of the Hertford Police has asked anyone with information on the whereabouts of Mrs Ashfield to come forward as soon as possible to help him with his investigation.

"I love Peter Higginsworth. I've read a couple of his books on haunted houses, and he really knows his stuff. We need to go there and film it. If that place made it into one of Higginsworth's books, then it's got to be haunted!" Kane gushed with newfound enthusiasm.

"Exactly!" JJ mumbled as he polished off the last piece of his donut and began licking his fingers.

Meanwhile, on the periphery of the buzz JJ had just injected, Zach sat hypnotized by the article and its pictures. He was a slower reader, being younger, but it didn't bother him. He always tried to commit everything to memory and retain it the same way his brother did.

Zach's concentration was broken by Kane leaping up from his chair as JJ's idea gained momentum in his mind.

He was really cooking now. This was just the inspiration he was looking for.

"We can go there today!" Kane shouted, "I bet the older kids only go there when it's dark, so we can have a good look around in the daytime, then post something when we get back."

JJ gave a sugary thumbs up in agreement.

"Let's go nowww!" pleaded Zach, as he tuned in to his brother's voice, his eyes not moving from the screen.

Before Kane could put up any form of protest, Zach reminded him, "Mum and dad are going shopping and then straight on to their date night, rememberrr? If you go, I go."

"Fine." Kane replied. "But you need to stay away from the camera and keep quiet when we're filming, ok?"

Zach looked wounded by his brother's conditions.

The puppy dog eyes threatened to make another appearance, when Kane added, "Otherwise we'll do it tomorrow on our own."

Zach dropped the pretence before it started and agreed to his brother's terms.

He wouldn't miss this for the world.

10

The boys were all hyped for their day of filming, speculating about all the things they might catch on camera while they prepared for their visit.

Cold Christmas was the adjoining village, a mere 20-minute walk from Kane's house in Shawbrook. Crooked House was said to be in the middle of a wooded area and quite secluded, but this only added to its eerie appeal.

JJ had already plotted their route on his phone whilst Kane had packed a rucksack full of sandwiches and snacks for them all.

They were ready.

In fact, they were in such a hurry to get on their way that they nearly steamrolled the two girls on the doorstep as they bundled out of the front door.

"Careful!" exclaimed Meridia. Her cheeks were almost as red as her hair, whilst her bright blue eyes scowled at the three boys now wedged firmly in the doorframe. "Zach Jackson, where are you off to in such a rush?!" she demanded as her glare softened a little and her composure returned.

Meridia Wilson was Zach's best friend and long-time crush. Aside from his brother and JJ, she was the coolest person he knew, and the prettiest. Meridia was wrapped up in her favourite green puffer jacket. The collar was up high, almost covering her mouth, whilst her long curls kept her ears warm. She may have looked delicate, but Meridia was fierce when she needed to be, and wasn't a girl to be trifled with.

Standing beside her was Izzy Di Salvo, unflustered by the jump-scare the boys had just served up. She looked at them inquisitively from behind her tortoiseshell glasses as if they had just beamed down from mars. Izzy was dressed immaculately, as always. She chose to play it down, but her dad was a top accountant in the city, so she often wore expensive designer clothes. To disguise this fact, Izzy insisted on wearing more low-key, neutral colours in order to blend in. Today's colour of choice was her favourite charcoal grey, which she felt complimented her mousey brown hair that she always tied back into a neat ponytail. She was a creature of habit and a bit of a wallflower.

"Hi James..." she bashfully murmured, but her meek voice was swallowed up by the kerfuffle.

Both Izzy and Meridia lived on the same street as Zach and were in his year group at school. Most people thought Izzy was the odd one out because of her more studious nature, but the three of them shared a keen interest in technology and went to coding classes together at lunchtime.

In all the excitement, Zach had forgotten they were both coming round to work on their latest project.

"Change of plans," Zach announced once he'd realized his diary clash. "We're going to explore a haunted hotel now instead!"

"Err, hang on a minute," Kane interrupted.

"Come on. It's perfect," protested Zach, stepping out of the congested doorframe to make his point. "This way I'll have my friends there to keep me out of your way, plus we can be your eyes and ears in all the places you're not filming to see if we find anything scary."

Kane glanced at JJ, who was pretending to study the route on his phone. He didn't want to get involved in any family politics, but could sense both brother's eyes boring into him.

Succumbing to the pressure, JJ looked their way and shrugged his shoulders.

"Makes no difference to me, mate." Kane surveyed the three kids in front of him and wrinkled one side of his face as if he was weighing up the proposition. As much as it pained him to admit it, Zach made a valid point, and any arguing would only delay them further from getting to Crooked House.

He wanted to get there now while the sun was shining, and his ideas were in full flow. Kane paced up and down the garden lawn for dramatic effect, as if still weighing up his options. The winter sun had melted away the morning frost, and his trainers squeaked on the glistening wet grass with every step he took.

The three gatecrashers watched on in silent anticipation as they tried to get a read on Kane's best poker face.

"Fine! You can all tag along." He snapped and then walked towards the garden gate. "You can fill your friends in on the way there," he added without looking back at any of them.

None of them had ever been to a haunted house before.

This was going to be epic.

II

"Are we there yet?" Zach complained as they trudged down the bland dual carriageway leading them out of Shawbrook.

"Quit whining mate, we only left the house ten minutes ago! Besides, you'll be begging to go home once we get there and the boogeyman tries to get his hands on you." Kane gave JJ a subtle wink as he led the pack in search of a hidden dirt track, which, according to Google Maps, would lead them straight to Crooked House.

"Wait..what boogeyman?!" Zach stammered, taking the bait.

"He's winding you up Zach. There's no such thing." Meridia chimed in, sensing the nervousness in Zach's voice.

"There's no smoke without fire. Crooked House has been one of the most haunted places in the country for years. They say the boogeyman murdered the owner there a few years ago, chopping him up into tiny pieces and burying him in the surrounding woods. Then, years later, his wife went missing too, and neither body has ever been found." Kane continued to turn the screw on his little brother.

"Wait, where did you hear that? That wasn't in the article! It just said they were missing..." Zach was now wriggling on the line and waiting to be reeled in.

"I read it on my phone whilst we've been walking. Just been doing a bit of extra research before we get there."

"Where? Show me!" Zach demanded as they left the main road for the narrow, dusty path Google had promised them.

"I'll have to show you later now. My signal just dropped. They say that's what happens when you get to this place...it's so you can't call for help when the boogeyman comes."

"JJ, have you got signal?" Zach was starting to worry as they continued to march over the frozen ground, hemmed in by decayed, greyed-out wooden fencing on either side.

"Don't listen to him." Meridia leapt to Zach's aid again. "He's just making it up to scare us...The boogeyman isn't real..."

Kane chuckled to himself, deciding to ease up on his gullible brother just as they reached the end of the path.

Ahead of them was a main road with a smattering of old wooden faced bungalows.

To their left was an old, crooked road sign which read *'Cold Christmas Lane'*.

"Welcome to Cold Christmas," JJ proclaimed. "Population: five."

"Is this it?" Meridia quibbled.

"Nah, we've got another dirt track to follow behind the village. It's in the middle of the woods, remember?" JJ pointed across the road to where the path resumed between two of the properties.

At first glance, Cold Christmas resembled a ghost town, with no real sign of life other than the odd handwritten sign propped up against a box or a basket where neighbours were hoping to sell their local produce. The houses were more shabby than chic, sporting broken fences and unkempt gardens, which had all the allure of a run-down council estate. The roadside also appeared completely deserted, with no cars or bikes in sight. It was as if they had stepped a hundred years back in time.

"We're five minutes out guys, so not much further now. It's literally just up ahead."

Crooked House was off the well-beaten path, framed by a smattering of oak and alder trees, its exterior was something from the pages of an age-old fairy tale. It had dusty pink walls and a rustic stone path, which cut a jagged walkway through the unkempt grass. Sash windows in a variety of different sizes completed the B&B's quaint, friendly appeal as they each reflected the surrounding trees. Almost completely hemmed in by woodland, its only link to the outside world came in the shape of a winding gravel path to the rear of the house which was barely a car's width.

As they all stepped into the clearing out front, Kane noticed the air seemed perfectly still, sheltered by the dense trees.

There was an eery silence despite the natural setting. No sound of animals or insects to be heard, no humming traffic in the distance. In fact, there was no sign of life at all. Crooked House could easily have been the home to Red Riding Hood's grandmother, or the wolf perhaps.

"Is it me or has the temperature just dropped?" Zach asked, as he exhaled a huge puff of air and watched it condense in front of him.

Unlike the slow thaw in Shawbrook, here there was a silver shimmer to the twigs and fallen branches scattered around them as if they had yet to see the sun.

"Well, we are in the middle of winter mate. Maybe that's why they call it Cold Christmas?" Kane quipped.

"It doesn't look very haunted or creepy though," Meridia declared as the group approached the front of the building. "It looks like a sweet old lady's house, only bigger."

"She's not wrong," Kane thought to himself as he stared at the giant pink building before him.

There was a pang of disappointment shared amongst the group. They had spent the entire walk there concocting images in their minds more akin to *Count Draculas'* castle than what they saw before them.

A gentle breeze, which weaved its way between them all like a snake, swiftly interrupted the anti-climax. The sudden burst of cold air made its way to an old wooden rocking chair which decorated the porch, setting it in motion with a loud *Creeeak!*

Zach and Meridia clung onto each other as they both jumped at the ominous sound.

"Very Evil Dead," Kane chuckled. The chair stopped abruptly in its tracks, as if objecting to his wisecrack. "Wish I'd got that on film now," he sighed to himself.

JJ chimed in to change the mood as he so often did whenever he sensed Kane was teetering on the brink of despondency.

"It's not about the outside guys, it's all about the inside!" he chirped, walking backwards towards the house as if to lure everyone closer to it. "It said online there's a loose board around the back so we can film inside. Apparently it's dead spooky." JJ's words hung in the air and for a second or two, stopping time in its tracks.

Things had just become real. A tingling, nervous energy brushed the back of Kane and Zach's necks, causing them to shudder in unison as if someone had walked over their graves. Despite the welcoming face of Crooked House, none of them knew what lurked inside its deserted, dust-filled rooms.

"Excellent!" Izzy broke the spell of silence. Her eyes lit up behind her glasses as she flashed a rare grin of anticipation.

Kane had always found Izzy a little odd. If someone told him she was a distant cousin of the Addams Family, he wouldn't have been the least bit surprised. He looked at her, puzzled and wondered how she and Meridia had ever become friends. Still, Izzy was super smart and her scepticism of anything paranormal might just help keep everyone else grounded when they got inside.

Kane shuddered again as the thought of going inside crystallized in his mind. As a precaution, he subtly checked his phone for a signal but found he had none whatsoever.

"Nothing to be scared about," he muttered to himself and rallied the troops in readiness for filming. It was show-time.

"So, the plan is we'll just keep the camera rolling and edit anything we need to when we get back this afternoon," Kane explained. "JJ will be behind the camera, and you three need to make sure you're not seen or heard." He emphatically looked at Zach.

Zach had a habit of being a chatterbox when he got excited, and Kane could see he was already brimming with enthusiasm.

The walk there had lit a fuse in his brother's imagination, and the soft, cuddly appearance of the house hadn't dampened it.

The three children all nodded in agreement with Kane's conditions and signalled the start of proceedings. However, in all the group's preparations to enter Crooked House, nobody noticed the perfectly still silhouette watching them from the window.

The daylight caught the shadowy figure's eyes, which seemed to defy the laws of physics. The two tiny glistening orbs were more than a mere reflection of the winter sun, they appeared to have their own power source from within, like Christmas tree lights.

Oblivious, the group gathered around the loose board covering the bottom half of the back door.

Kane bent the panel back with a tiny groan, and one by one they all disappeared inside.

12

Despite its many windows, Crooked House was dark inside. It was also deceptively large. Stifled rays of sunlight peppered the empty halls, revealing thousands of tiny dust particles dancing around in excitement as they welcomed their latest guests in with open arms. There was a faint smell of cat wee upon entry and child-like graffiti on the wall closest to the back door they had just entered. The abandoned building had an unmistakably creepy quality to it, but it was masterfully disguised by the soft pink walls and pretty plant pots outside.

"This is more like it," Kane beamed.

JJ turned his cap round backwards, so it didn't obstruct his view, and then switched the camera light on to help everyone get their bearings.

"Aaaah!" Meridia's scream echoed along the empty corridor, causing everyone to leap out of their skin.

"What?! What is it?" Zach gasped as Meridia pointed a shaky finger towards the floor.

JJ's light had bounced off a headless pigeon in front of them; its sparsely feathered corpse lay directly at their feet.

"Well, the ghosts definitely know we're here now!" Kane said sarcastically whilst pretending to unblock his ringing ear with a finger.

"Don't worry," added Izzy, "that'll just be the cat we can smell. They often bring in trophies for their owners."

"I wonder who its owner could be here?" Kane mused, half playing up to the camera. It was a valid point and caused everyone to pause in contemplation.

"Wait, what if someone is actually living here?" Meridia asked with hesitation.

"Or something?" Kane added, now revelling in his role as entertainer. He turned to the camera and added, "As you might have guessed by the girly scream you heard, my younger brother Zach is here with us today, and he's brought along some of his friends." Kane gestured towards the three gate crashers the way a cheesy game show host unveils a booby prize.

JJ responded and scanned the awkward faces with his camera, half blinding them with his spotlight.

Kane figured he had nothing to lose now, so might as well give today's post everything he could. After all, almost all his followers were now crammed together in the same narrow hallway as him. *"If you can't beat 'em, join 'em,"* he thought.

Kane stepped over the headless pigeon and assumed what he felt was his rightful place at the front of the group. He was the face of *Scarytales* in fairness, and JJ much preferred staying behind the lens. He lowered his voice to a whisper and looked directly into the camera.

"We are now about to enter the living room of Crooked House, or more like the dead room. Rumour has it this place has been haunted for 300 years thanks to countless sightings of mysterious figures and ghostly apparitions.

Who knows, we may even be lucky enough to see Percy, the headless pigeon, who is said to occasionally walk the halls at night..."

Zach sniggered from the back of the group. Even when Kane wasn't on his best form, he hung on his every word. He idolized his brother.

The narrow hall led into the much wider space Kane had alluded to, so he made way for JJ to capture the area with his camera. Their surroundings were far darker now as they moved closer to the centre of the building. All the windows to the rear were locked away behind closed guest room doors, so they had no idea what might be waiting between them and the faint light they could see coming from the opposite end.

The light from JJ's camera revealed a make-shift mahogany service bar which separated the kitchen area from the lounge. There were two dusty glasses on the bar, empty, as if a couple of ghosts had met there for drinks one evening. Old newspapers and magazines were littered around the coffee table and floor next to a green, and rather plush looking, suede armchair. A sofa occupied the far-right corner. It was a dirty yellow and missing some of its cushions. Next to that was a rounded coffee table which had been overturned, casting a peculiar shadow on the wall when the light hit it.

For a moment, JJ mistook it for a crouching figure in the corner of the room.

"What the f..." His hand trembled in fright, causing the light to skip and dance uncontrollably.

"What?! What is it?!" Meridia shrieked, panicked by the fearful look on JJ's face.

After a moment's hesitation, he retraced his last couple

of steps as his brain scrambled to make sense of what he'd just seen.

"Just a trick of the light," he reassured himself and continued his exploration. Framing the living space were several rooms. The far-right corner had a bold '*OFFICE*' sign and a large frosted glass door to its right.

As the light cut through another troupe of dancing dust particles, the vague silhouette of a rocking chair could be seen on the other side.

"That has to be the front of the building," JJ clarified.

He slowly shifted his camera's attention back to the left now and revealed a series of closed doors which were identical aside from their numbers. Panning counter clockwise, he read each number aloud "1...2...3...4...5..."

His light then darted back down the narrow hallway they had just came from, catching Percy's headless corpse again along the way.

JJ knew there were ten rooms in total from his research, so he continued his journey left and revealed the number 6 as expected. Almost in response to being seen, the door softly clicked and drifted ajar with a slow *creak*.

JJ's hand shook with fear, bringing the brass number 6 to life as it jumped and danced around in the trembling spotlight.

A warm blanket of anxiety smothered everyone, as they realized they were not alone.

The group huddled together on red alert. The risk they had taken going inside Crooked House suddenly hit them all like a sledgehammer. However, their first thoughts were not of a ghost or shadowy spectre, but of a real-life person whose home they may have just invaded.

"H...hello" Kane stuttered, "is there any...anyone there?" his choice of words could have been a plucked from any eighties horror movie and left him feeling like a total amateur.

Meridia and Zach instinctively clasped hands as they anxiously waited for a reply. The warmth of her palm pressed against his, sent his heart racing even faster as he tried his best to play it cool.

All five were frozen in place.

They all held their breath for a lifetime while JJ tried to keep his shaky camera light focused on the door to room 6.

The silence was deafening until JJ began to creep closer to the open door in a slow, yet impulsive manner.

Kane tried to grab his arm and hold him back as he passed, but JJ wriggled free and gave an assured gesture before bravely edging his way even further forward.

"It's just a cat," he repeated to himself over and over with every tiny step he made, "it's just a cat...that knows how to open doors." As he got within touching distance of the room, JJ's heart rate increased momentarily. He slowly raised his free hand to push the door open, being sure to stay at arm's length from whatever may be waiting for him on the other side. Just as his clammy hand was about to make contact, the light on his camera flickered and threatened to go out. "Shit!" He froze for a moment, but the light stabilized again. Letting out a sigh of relief, he decided it was now or never.

JJ gave the door a firm shove and immediately stepped back, all the while trying his best to keep the light focused on the space in front of him.

The door swung away from him at speed, almost as if someone was pulling on the other side trying to get out. His light bolted into the cavity beyond the open door and that was when they all saw it.

A shockwave of fear surged throughout the group as

they instinctively gripped onto each other for dear life. JJ's camera shook as adrenalin coursed through his veins in readiness to tackle the abomination that was waiting for them all in room 6.

Far more terrifying than any boogeyman they could have conjured up, they had come to Crooked House in search of adventure, but what they had found was pure evil.

A tall figure of pure rage was standing in the middle of the room, staring at them through burning white pupils, which scorched their way through the darkness. Its skin seemed immune to JJ's trembling light and remained unnaturally vague, as if it was out of focus. It glared at the five intruders with unblinking, demented eyes and began to hiss at them through jagged teeth gritted together like a wild dog's. Making a stance as if it was about to pounce at the open door, the creature let out a high-pitched scream and coiled its legs back in readiness to attack. Long thin talons caught the dancing light as it raised its arms, ready to strike.

Panic filled the air as JJ's hands tremored, holding the dancing light, before he turned and bolted towards the door, as if fleeing a burning building.

"RUN!!" he bellowed.

Light bounced around the narrow hallway to a chorus of heavy, frantic footsteps which reverberated off the stony ground, turning Crooked House into an echo chamber as the children collided with each other and the walls in their desperation to escape. In a frenzy, they screamed and fumbled in search of an exit.

Trying his best not to trip over Izzy's flailing legs, JJ followed the pack as they rattled their way down a dark corridor.

"KEEP GOING!" he cried, but his light couldn't

penetrate the fleeing herd in front of him to see where they were all headed.

The surrounding air rapidly became dense and hot as everyone puffed and panted in their panic, sucking the oxygen out of the B&B's airtight remains.

Meridia felt herself leaning further and further forward into the void between her and Kane as she sprinted to keep up. She was about to lose all control and tumble to the ground when Kane suddenly stopped, leaving her no choice but to collide into the back of him.

As the rest of the convoy concertinaed together, it became clear, they had reached an unexpected dead end.

"Where's the exit?!" Meridia shrieked, squashed between both Jackson brothers, as the group tried to force their way out.

"I can't see a thing," Zach whimpered in frustration, "Where's JJ?"

Overcome with terror, JJ's light moved too quickly at first, flashing past anything and everything in their vicinity, until he gripped the camera with both hands in order to steady himself.

"Nooo!" cried Kane as the words 'OFFICE' greeted him and he realized their panic had led them to the wrong side of the building!

If they wanted to get out alive, they would need to go back where they came from and somehow get past the monster in room 6.

JJ spun around and frantically sprayed his light in every direction to search the open space around them.

There was no obvious exit, just a dark, endless corridor to their left.

They were trapped.

Zach forced his way through the group towards JJ. He was crying now, "We've got to go back," he sobbed.

JJ accommodated cautiously, deciding it was safer to point the camera at the floor in front of them and nudge it further and further in the direction of room 6. Filled with dread, he could feel his heart thumping in his chest as the light edged closer and closer to the ominous room.

The luminous wave swept across the kitchen counter, catching two glistening orbs in the shadows that looked like the monster's eyes.

JJ suddenly felt hot, as if he was about to pass out, but his brain overruled his imagination and reassured him they were just the empty glasses he'd seen earlier. He let out the breath he'd been holding and continued to push onward, expecting at any moment to see something terrifying. It took all his strength to push and nudge the light along, but there were no bright burning eyes to welcome him.

No shadowy figure charging at them. There was nothing, only silence.

The beam just about stretched to the bottom of the door to room 6 but something was different. It was closed again, exactly as it was when they first arrived.

"What now?" Meridia whispered as they stood huddled together by the frosted porch door.

They all looked at each other in expectation, hoping someone might have an answer.

Izzy's eyes began performing a slalom from left to right as if she was speed reading something in front of her. She was busy assessing their options.

"It could have been a trick of the light," she opened with. "Just a cat, or some other kind of animal that's been trapped in here."

"That...that was no cat!" JJ countered defensively.

"That was something else...evil...just pure evil!" His hands were still shaking from fear as he tried to erase the creature's hideous face from his memory.

"But it is dark, and we're all excited," Izzy pressed. "The mind can play tricks, and besides, where is it now?" She sounded firmer in her belief, as if she was reassuring herself whilst talking it through.

"No way!" JJ argued, "We all saw that...that thing! It was no damn cat!"

Izzy could tell she was annoying him, but they needed a plan to escape.

"I think we should form a circle, with our backs to each other and work our way back out of here as quick as we can. That way nothing can sneak up on us." Izzy's plan was as good as any Kane could think of, and they couldn't just stand there waiting for something else to happen–they were sitting ducks.

"Let's do it," he said in agreement, and they all got into formation, locking arms to help keep their shape.

After a lot of deep breaths and anxious squeezing of hands, they shuffled slowly and awkwardly back towards the dreaded room 6.

Crooked House was still and silent as it was when they first arrived, as if nothing had ever happened. The eerie quiet amplified the soft scraping of rubber soles against the stony ground, providing the baseline to a tune of shallow breathing as they carved their way across the living space.

Being careful not to bundle into his escort, JJ assumed the role of a mobile lighthouse to flush out anything that might be lurking in the surrounding shadows.

When they reached room 6 Kane pulled them all to an abrupt halt.

"Shhh! Can you hear that?" A faint, muffled noise was

escaping from behind the door. It was a soft sound, a million miles from the threatening hissing and screaming they had all heard moments ago.

Kane closed his eyes in an attempt to hone in on it.

"Sobbing," he whispered. "It sounds like someone's crying in there."

This presented them with an entirely new dilemma, given they were only a few metres from escape. Breadcrumbs of light peppered the dark path back to the loose board they'd broken in through. It was their makeshift exit sign, and it was beckoning them to make a run for it. However, behind the door of room 6 was the sound of someone in trouble who needed their help.

"We can't leave," Meridia said in a soft but firm voice. "Someone might be hurt."

"What if it's a trap?" Zach countered nervously.

"Obviously it's a trap!" Izzy replied deadpan.

"What? We're gonna need a weapon then." Zach was becoming more frightened with each exchange.

"Did anyone bring a gun with them? Cause that's the only thing that's going to convince me to step foot in that room again." JJ was only half joking as he moved his light around in search of something, anything, they could use. "Where's the conveniently placed lump of wood or brick they always find in horror films?"

Alas, there was nothing even remotely useful to them. All the while, the sobbing continued, like a ticking pressure-clock urging them to make a decision.

Kane took a deep breath and tipped the balance of their quandary, "I'm going to look."

He let go of his brother's hand and stretched his arm out in front of him until his palm was firmly pressed against the smooth painted wood of the door. Like a slinky, the rest of his body played catch-up until he could cup his ear and eavesdrop. He listened intently to the steady sobbing. Thankfully, there was no hissing or growling accompanying it. All he could hear was what sounded like a child in some sort of pain. He gripped the door handle and took another deep breath for courage.

He trembled, grappling with his fears of what awaited him beyond the door.

Just as he was about to lose that battle and chicken-out altogether, he felt JJ arrive next to him. He went shoulder to shoulder as an unspoken sign of solidarity. It was just the lift Kane needed, and so he carefully turned the handle, trying his best not to make a sound.

The door gave a gentle *creak* as Kane slowly pushed it open.

JJ's light filled the cavity of the open room, but this time there was no shadowy monster staring back at them. At first glance, the room looked empty. Across the unmade bed in the middle was a window with firmly drawn blackout curtains. At the foot of the bed, a dusty mahogany dressing table completed the modest-looking décor. Both Kane and JJ breathed a deep sigh of relief, and then they noticed him.

"Shit!" Kane grabbed onto JJ's arm in shock, spreading his panic like wildfire and welding them both to the spot.

Crouched in the corner was a small boy in a dirty blue hoodie. The boy had his back facing them, and his head was hung low as if he had fallen asleep. Narrow shoulders gently rocked, cajoling each new sob to the surface.

He seemed to be muttering something to himself, but it wasn't quite audible.

The boy seemed oblivious to the spotlight he was now under, so Kane and JJ ventured beyond the doorway and into the room.

They needed to hear what he was mumbling. "Air falcon?" thought Kane as he took another couple of steps closer, "What the hell does that mean?"

"They're all gone.... they're all gone." The boy's strange chant came sharply into focus.

"Who are all gone?" Kane thought to himself as he plucked up the courage to speak aloud. "Hey," he squeaked, "are you ok?"

The mysterious boy stopped muttering to himself immediately. The last dregs of a sob escaped him, followed by a loud '*sniff*' as he appeared to regain some composure.

"Hey," Kane repeated in his best comforting voice, "it's ok, we're not going to hurt you."

The boy started sobbing again and hurriedly shuffled his body round to face everyone.

Kane was the first to catch sight of the boy's face and his odd reaction baffled the rest of the group as they eagerly watched on. Kane's eyes showed a mix of confusion and terror as they immediately darted towards Zach, who was firmly wedged between JJ and Meridia in the doorway.

A wave of dread rippled its way across the group as they froze in nervous anticipation of another nasty surprise.

"What is it?" Meridia whispered, desperate to know what was going on.

Her words hung in the air, unanswered for what seemed like an eternity until Kane let out a befuddled gasp and redirected his attention back to the hooded boy in the corner.

BANG!

He reeled backwards suddenly, crashing into the dresser behind him. The wooden frame rocked on its legs, echoing in the sparse room as it clattered against the wall.

The sudden noise proved the perfect vessel to carry

Kane's panic to the rest of the group, who for what felt like the umpteenth time that day all found themselves frozen to the spot.

JJ's light caught the boy's jawline as he turned.

His appearance matched his dirty hoody, as if he had found his way in through the chimney. He lifted his arms and pulled his hood down to reveal a face awash with dirt and despair. His wavy brown fringe clung to his head, giving the impression that he hadn't showered in a month. Underneath, his dark eyes gleamed eerily, resembling the strange monster they had encountered earlier. A dry-mouthed silence swept across the room as they ogled the boy in disbelief.

"Z..Zach?" Meridia gasped, as the soot-covered doppelgänger's sobbing turned to anger and frustration as he shouted,

"YOU'RE ALL GONE!... WE LOST!....WE LOST THE INVISIBLE WAR!... IT'S OVER!"

And with that, a strange orb of brilliant white light appeared from behind him and began rapidly circling the room. The entire building seemed to vibrate as the light got stronger and stronger, blinding everyone in its wake. As it grew more intense, the cries of the hooded imposter morphed into a deafening high-pitched whistle.

An ornate China tea-set rattled off the wooden dresser and toppled to the ground, smashing into tiny pieces next to the bed. A rustic-looking vanity mirror soon followed, leaping off the wall and shattering violently as it struck the slate flooring behind Kane. The pandemonium intensified, feeling like the very fabric of reality was being ripped in two.

Then everything stopped abruptly.

The room was still, and the boy was gone.

13

A CHORUS OF SCREAMS BROKE OUT: TERRIFIED, confused screams that reverberated through Crooked House as if it was home to a high-octane fairground ride.

Nobody knew what to do next.

Unsure of what he'd seen, Zach stood deathly still in a state of shock whilst the rest of the group danced around him like headless chickens. As the bedlam unfolded around him, a hundred questions flooded his frazzled brain as he tried to process what he'd just seen.

"How can this be happening? That was me...in the room...but I'm here. God, my eyes...was it a ghost? Am I going to die in here? Please God, don't let me die in here..." The sound of broken glass crackling underfoot snapped Zach out of his trance and he followed the others as they bolted their way back towards the open door.

Meridia and Izzy were forced apart and swept back into the hallway in a tidal wave of panic. As she drifted beyond the doorway, Meridia thought she heard something.

"Meridia..." The whisper was faint at first, but enough to stop her in her tracks. It came again, this time undeniably.

"Meridiaaaa..." She shook her head, bewildered, as she surveyed the barren room behind her.

"Must have been Izzy in all the confusion," she thought. But it didn't sound like Izzy, and she was sure it had come from the wardrobe in the corner. Before she had time to give it any more thought, Kane cut across her with deadpan authority.

"We're leaving!"

The group immediately hurried down the hallway as JJ's camera flitted from side-to-side checking for anything that might try to stop them.

They were at the loose panel in a matter of seconds and Kane pushed it forward for everyone to squeeze their way out, one by one. He took one last bemused look back down the hall, still trying to process what he'd seen, then he followed everyone out into the crisp winter air.

The sunlight was blinding as their eyes adjusted from the gloom they had narrowly escaped.

The icy breeze that greeted them carried quite the bite, stinging their lungs and prickling their cheeks as they tried to catch their breath.

"Keep going," Kane insisted, gesturing towards the woods, but nobody needed any encouragement.

They ran as fast as their trembling legs would carry them, pushing Crooked House as far behind them as possible. Eventually they reached Jubilee Park, which sat between Kane's house and Cold Christmas. As the park's gates and open field came into sight, they all shifted gears to a jog, then slowed to a brisk walk.

All five of them bundled onto an old graffitied bench they had claimed as their own over the years and desperately tried to catch their breath. It was just another Saturday in the park as children enjoyed the play area in the distance. The frosty reception of Cold Christmas was a distant memory as thick green grass glistened under the winter sun.

A toddler ambled past slightly ahead of his doting dad. He was chasing pigeons without a care in the world.

"We're safe now," JJ reassured them all. He removed his cap and wiped the sweat from his forehead as he tried to gather himself.

Scared out of their wits, they had sprinted the best part of a mile and were exhausted.

Meridia took a moment to absorb the scenery, as if it was her first time seeing it. The meandering asphalt path was sprinkled with cyclists circling the plush green football field, whilst a distant row of dense bushes she had played amongst with her father were now nothing more than thorny skeletons of a summer dream. Somewhere in the distance of the group's silent reflection, she could hear the familiar squeak of her favourite swing as it rhythmically swayed back and forth in the children's playground. She'd been to the park hundreds, if not thousands of times, but she'd never been so glad to be there as she was now.

The familiarity of the place soothed her.

It was predictable.

It was 'safe' just as JJ had said.

"What just happened?!" JJ's voice dragged her away from the comfort blanket she was busily knitting in her mind. His question was aimed at anyone listening.

They'd all just had the fright of their lives and although they were out of danger, their adrenalin was still pumping. There was no explaining any of it. Whilst they'd all hoped for a supernatural experience that day, nothing could have prepared them for the abomination they had just witnessed in room 6.

"Please tell me you recorded that, James." Izzy exclaimed.

Finding nicknames a struggle, Izzy always insisted on calling everyone by their official birth name. It was the tip of the iceberg in her long list of social hang-ups, but they only made her all the more endearing to the group. Izzy was the only person who ever called JJ by his real name 'James', and she was the only person JJ didn't object to doing so.

"I got the whole thing," JJ declared with pride. "The screen on this thing is pretty small though, so I think we should go look at what we've got somewhere else." He glanced up at Kane, who was tightly wound and anxiously pacing back and forth in front of the bench.

His eyes never wandered far from his kid brother, who was sitting at the very end, dejected, and staring at the ground in his own private daze.

"Let's go back to mine in that case," Kane replied. "Our parents will be out shopping late, so we can all look at the footage together and decide what to do with it."

The younger members of the group felt a sense of relief at hearing Kane's plan. It made them feel included, which was reassuring given they had pretty much gate-crashed his party that day. Nodding in agreement, they all picked themselves up off the bench and made the ten-minute walk to the Jackson house in self-reflective silence.

Kane kept a reassuring arm around his younger brother the entire way back.

Zach had the most questions from today's events, and Kane could only imagine how scared and confused he was by it all.

A cloud of apprehension descended on the group as Kane's house came into view and they began to question any desire to commemorate their brush with Crooked

House on the small screen. The walk back allowed them to regain composure and they were now protective of it.

Meridia's apprehension turned to dread at the sound of Kane's front door key turning in the lock.

The sound transported her back to the lock on room 6 and she shuddered a little as they all stepped inside.

14

Kane's bedroom was tidy and well organized. He was a minimalist when it came to furniture, so everything was hidden away except for his TV and a laptop, which sat perpendicular on his desk. Had it not been for the numerous horror movie posters on his walls, it might have been mistaken for a show-home.

As the group entered, they couldn't help but notice how comical the posters looked compared to what they had just experienced. Ghost-faced killers and hockey masked madmen had nothing on the creature they had encountered at Crooked House.

Whatever they had seen today looked like it had clawed its way out of the depths of hell.

All Zach could think about were its eyes shining in the dark. He had never felt so terrified in his life, and his mind spiralled out of control. *"What would happen if the monster followed them back to their homes and now knows where they live? Imagine if it came to take him while he slept at night? What if he never slept again?"* The questions kept pouring in as he sat down on his brother's bed. Although he was in his own house now, he felt a million miles from safety.

JJ entered after using the bathroom and went straight to work, connecting his camera to the TV as if on autopilot. The two friends had perfected their routine for reviewing and posting video content in the past month. He selected the last file on his camera and pressed play.

JJ was about to skip past the external shot he captured when they first arrived at the loose board, but Zach stopped him and pointed at the corner of the screen.

"Wait! Look there!" he shouted.

Over Kane's left shoulder, to the right of the board, there was a small child staring into the camera from inside one of the rooms.

JJ rewound the video and paused it to get a better look.

Someone was there, but it was hard to see due to the video being out of focus and the figure hidden behind curtains.

"It looks like the Amityville ghost," Kane declared. "It's a famous photo of a haunting in America. I can't believe we got that on film!" he pulled a piece of paper and pen out of the top drawer of his desk and began to sketch the layout of Crooked House.

"Based on where that little kid is in relation to where we entered, that has to be room 6." Kane concluded, waving his map around so everyone could see.

JJ and Izzy both concurred with Kane's logic and gave him a brief nod.

"But who is it, and where did they disappear to when we went in?"

The group studied the static image as if waiting for the child in the frame to answer Kane's question. It remained quiet on the matter.

"Let's keep watching and see what else we've got," suggested Meridia impatiently. She was tired and just wanted to be back at home with her mum.

As JJ released his camera's hold on the mystery child, Kane wrote neatly on the back of his piece of paper '*Kid?*'.

The group watched on, mesmerized as the video unfolded in front of their eyes. Everything was happening exactly as they had remembered it, but it was far darker in the video, which made it difficult to make out any real detail. Between the poor lighting and JJ's shaky camera work, it was impossible to get a still image of the creature they had seen in room 6. JJ paused and rewound several times, but nothing seemed to help. One thing was for sure though, whatever that thing was, it was definitely not a cat.

"Do you think someone pranked us?" Izzy probed. "Did anyone else know you were going there?"

"I didn't tell anyone," JJ replied defensively. "I found the place online last night and didn't tell anyone until I got here."

"What about you, Kane?"

"I didn't have time. Besides, that would have been some prank to find someone who looks like..." Kane's sentence trailed off as he looked at Zach. "*God knows what must be going through his little mind*," he thought with more than a touch of guilt.

"Let's skip to my bit," Zach said, sensing the elephant in the room. Scared and confused by what had happened, he was equally curious to find out how the 'other Zach' looked, and sounded just like him. His mind was overloaded with imaginary scenarios, ranging from time travel to alien body snatchers.

He just wanted answers to quieten the noise in his head.

"Maybe seeing that bit again will help?" he added, doing his best to put on a brave face.

The run down the hallway was straight from the reels of a found footage movie, and whilst it certainly captured the atmosphere they'd experienced at the time, it told them nothing they didn't already know–they were all petrified. The reluctant journey back towards the room was equally unhelpful. It was far too dark to see anything, and JJ aiming the camera at the floor as he did would not win any Oscars for best camera work.

Kane wasn't sure which encounter he found more disturbing–the close call with the savage-looking monster, or the sight of his brother's identical twin, which he knew he didn't have.

When they reached the part of the video showing Kane open the door to the hooded boy in the corner, they could all clearly hear the sobbing on camera. However, as the boy turned to face them, there seemed to be some kind of static interference with the video recording.

A white pixelated haze blurred everything on the screen as if they were watching an exposé trying to protect the boy's identity.

"What did he mean by 'invisible war'?" Zach asked.

The group sat in dumfounded silence whilst JJ kept fast-forwarding and rewinding in the hope the interference might miraculously clear. Sadly, the video sequence had provided them with no new answers. There was no logical explanation for any of it. As far as any of them knew, ghosts were of the dead, not the living. Even Kane, with his extensive knowledge of horror lore, was stumped.

"Let's keep watching," he answered in defeat.

The camera recovered its clarity as they were all fleeing the B&B.

JJ must have been unaware he was still recording, as all he seemed focused on was the floor behind him. The very last shot on film was upside down looking backwards as Crooked House swayed from side to side in time with the rhythm of JJ's running.

"There they are again!" cried Zach.

JJ paused the video, revealing a far clearer image of the mysterious child in room 6, despite it being the wrong way up. Everyone in the room tilted their heads upside down to adjust to the screen in front of them.

Meridia burst out laughing at how silly they all must have looked. It instantly eased the tension that had been hanging over them since they'd started watching.

"Hang on a sec," JJ said as he took a screenshot of the image and then rotated it on the big screen so everyone could see.

Pressed against the window of room 6 was a little girl.

She looked a lot younger than anyone in the group, and at first glance she appeared quite normal. Wearing a grubby yellow summer dress that had seen better days, she had long tousled mousy hair, which was loosely swept to one side.

JJ zoomed in a little closer on the girl, who couldn't have been more than 6 years old. Upon closer inspection, she shared the same dark starlit eyes as the creature and the 'other Zach'. The look of anguish on her face was haunting.

"What is it with this place?" JJ voiced his exasperation.

Meanwhile, Meridia gazed at the screen along with the rest of the group. The girl's eyes had an eerie, hypnotic effect, as if they were reflecting her gaze. The conversation that followed between JJ and Kane slowed, grinding to a sluggish background drone as she glazed over and lost focus.

A faint whisper danced above the static and tiptoed into Meridia's ears.

The voice was melodic and enchanting as it called out to her.

"*Meridia... Meridia...*" Everyone else in the room was still and silent, as if they had been placed on pause, like the girl on the screen. Meridia grew drowsy as the voice continued to call out to her.

"*Come back.... come back Meridia... help me....*" The voice echoed in Merida's mind as if she was dreaming whilst the image on the screen began to flicker and move.

It started subtly, with just a twitch or two, but before she knew it the little girl in room 6 was a blur of frenzied motion as if she were wrestling to break free from a strait jacket. Despite her erratic movement, the girl's eyes remained unflinching and stayed locked on Meridia while she jostled within the walls of her TV prison. Her anguished look intensified, and her mouth hung open as if she was about to let out an enormous yawn. The little girl's jaw extended wider and wider as she moved beyond the confines of the TV screen, invading Kane's bedroom.

Paralyzed by fear, Meridia could do nothing but watch in terror as the ghostly child towered over her, all the while her mouth widening like a snake about to devour its prey.

Trembling, Meridia tried with all her might to alert her friends of the oncoming spectre, but her body wouldn't listen.

A solitary tear trickled down her cheek as she silently wrestled with all her concentration to break free from whatever spell she now found herself under, but it was all in vain.

Darkness engulfed the room and swallowed Meridia whole.

15

The next sound Meridia heard as she awoke was screaming.

The screaming pierced the dull ringing in her ears, which was left over from whatever nightmare she had just experienced. It took a couple of seconds for her brain-fog to subside before she realized the screams that filled the room were, in fact, her own.

She bolted upright, with a jump. The sudden rush of blood to her head made everything spin around her. She realized she was on the floor, but this wasn't Kane's room where she was moments ago.

This room was dark and dusty, yet it smelled familiar to her. The stale air carried a faint musty odour of old wood, but the feelings it stirred up in her were not those of childhood nostalgia, but ones of fear and dread. She had been there before.

Meridia felt something wet on the ground beside her and raised her hand to see what it was.

In the dim light, she could see a jagged piece of ornate china sticking out of her palm.

She winced at the stabbing pain which followed and pulled it out.

A cold sweat broke out across her forehead as blood trickled down her hand and slithered up her sleeve.

Meridia knew exactly where she was.

Looking up as her blurry eyes tried to adjust to their new surroundings, she could see the soot-covered little girl from the video footage, her eyes sparkling in the dark.

"You have to help me," she whispered, *"it won't let me leave."*

Meridia began screaming again; she couldn't stop herself.

Up close, the girl was the stuff of nightmares. Her skin was deathly pale under a layer of ash that dusted her from head to toe. Her face was covered with matted, dirty-looking long mousy hair, as if she'd just clambered her way out from her own grave. But it was her eyes that were particularly unsettling. Black, glassy orbs with luminous white pupils, like stars on a clear night.

She stared at Meridia unblinking.

With her head bowed towards the ground, Meridia shuffled away on her back like a crab to create a safe distance from the disturbing image confronting her, doing all she could to avoid the girl's haunting gaze. Around her, the dust filled room looked exactly as they had left it earlier.

There was no savage monster.

No mysterious replica of her best friend.

It was just her and the unearthly child with raven eyes.

Meridia found the courage to stop screaming and took a deep breath.

"Who won't let you leave?" she begged as calmly as her nerves would let her.

The girl pointed at the rustic oak wardrobe in the opposite corner.

"*The monster...*" A knot formed in the pit of Meridia's stomach as the little girl slowly walked over to where she was pointing. "*It's coming. I can feel it.*"

The back of Meridia's head touched the door behind her with a faint bump. She'd now put as much space between her and the girl as the room allowed. The thought of making a run for it crossed her mind, but she was still too groggy.

"What does it want?" she pressed, buying more time to recover.

"*It wants to...*" the girl paused and looked to her right as if an imaginary friend had just stopped her from leaking a secret. "*It wants to...*"

She took a half step forward. Her mouth opened to form a word, but nothing came out.

Fear gripped her.

Meridia instinctively wanted to comfort the strange child but couldn't find the strength to move.

"*It's coming.*" The girl's words marched to the forefront of her mind and dragged her back to reality.

"*It's here...*"

For the briefest moment, time slowed in anticipation of something horrifying, before returning to full speed again as the wardrobe door burst open, nearly breaking off its brass hinges.

A grizzly, gnarled hand, with twisted, sharp fingernails, reached out from the darkness and grabbed the girl viciously by the top of her arm. There was a brief struggle as the girl tried to wriggle free, like a mischievous toddler trying to elude their parent.

An unwilling spectator, Meridia squirmed, digging her

heels into the stony ground and forcing her back even further into the wall behind her until she could feel her spine creak under the pressure.

The little girl screamed, shrill with terror, before the menacing hand responded with a show of dominance, yanking her into the wardrobe with ferocious, superhuman force.

The heavy wooden door slammed firmly shut behind them.

16

Zach shook his head and blinked deliberately for a couple of seconds. He must've been staring too hard at the screen in his quest for answers. His eyes were suddenly dry and sore.

Kane and JJ were busy hypothesizing about Crooked House and the girl in the video.

Izzy was observing them as if she was watching a tennis match, her head intently following the flight of the conversation.

Zach turned toward Meridia and whispered, "Well, it's no worse than the Blair Witch and look how much money that made..." but Meridia was no longer next to him. His hand traced the edge of the bed she had been perched on, as if he doubted his own eyes. The duvet was warm to the touch where she had been sitting, but Meridia was nowhere to be seen.

"Where did Meridia go?" he interrupted.

Kane and JJ both looked dumbstruck at the empty space next to Zach. They didn't see anyone leave the room, and the only way out was past Kane by the door. Both boys were puzzled as JJ lifted his cap to scratch his head. Before they could utter a word of explanation, Izzy cut across them more animated than they had ever seen her.

"Oh my god, look!" she cried, pointing at the frozen image on the screen.

Behind the little girl, amongst the shadows of room 6, stood Meridia. She was mid-scream and her bright blue eyes were wide and filled with terror.

"We have to go get her!" Zach fumed as he leapt up. Tears welled within his scowling eyes as he soaked up Meridia's chilling expression. "We have to go right now!" He was frightened, but above all angry; angry at the house and angry at himself for failing to notice she'd gone.

Kane placed a hand on each of his brother's shoulders and gave him a gentle shake to snap his attention away from the screen. "It's going to be ok. We'll get her back, I promise."

"Shouldn't we call her mum...or the police?" JJ countered.

"And tell them what? A ghost kidnapped Meridia? They'll throw us in a loony bin! No we need to go back and fix all this. We should never have gone to that bloody place to begin with!" Kane now shared his brother's anger.

"Well, if we're going back to Crooked House, then we should think about posting the video before we leave." JJ added as he waved the camera around to emphasize his point. "That way, if anything happens to us, people will know where to look."

"What people? All our followers are in this room! Sorry...you're right. We can take it down again when we get back. No harm, no foul. It's not like anyone will see it unless they go looking. Any objections?"

Izzy and Zach both shrugged in agreement, so Kane gave JJ the nod and he set about his work.

"While that's uploading, I'll grab a few things for the trip. Something tells me we're gonna need more than sandwiches this time."

17

Crooked House had lost all its fairy-tale charm as the group approached it for the second time that day.

The soft pink walls were now scuffed and cracked as they struggled to contain the sinister forces operating within. Its unkempt garden was now littered with fallen branches and the debris from smashed plant pots, whilst the old rocking chair was toppled on its side as a strong breeze circled the group in search of their missing friend.

There was no time to waste; Meridia was in trouble, and the clock was ticking. They only had another couple of hours of daylight, and none of them wanted to be anywhere near this place come nightfall. This time, however, they had come more prepared.

"Meridia! Meridia! Meridia!" Kane shouted as they approached, but the blustery wind seemed to swallow every one of his calls, reducing them to a pathetic whisper.

The trees around the entrance bowed under the force of the breeze, which was rapidly whipping its way up to a gale since their arrival. It was as if some invisible force didn't want them to enter.

The group doggedly made their way to the back of the building, where the loose board was waiting for them.

Kane pulled the splintered, weather-beaten panel back and held it firm. One by one they entered, camera, torches, and weapons at the ready. The wooden board snapped shut behind them and the sound of the stormy wind came to an abrupt halt.

JJ started filming again as they entered the narrow hallway. In his other hand was a well-worn and slightly chipped cricket bat he'd 'borrowed' from Kane's dad.

Izzy and Zach were both armed with torches and were under strict instructions to run at the first sign of any trouble.

Meanwhile, Kane was bringing up the rear with a shiny blue hockey stick his parents had bought him last Christmas to lure him away from his obsession with watching horror movies. Needless to say, Kane had never used it and it was still covered in saran wrap.

Everything was quiet and still in the B&B, just as it was during their first visit.

"You came..." the melodic whisper echoed down the hall towards them.

"Meridia?!"

"Meridia?!" they all called out into the gloom as they followed the haunting voice in the direction of room 6.

"What the hell are we doing here?" JJ begged. "I mean, what are we going to do if that...that thing comes back? Challenge it to a game of cricket?" Crooked House was the last place they expected to be again so soon.

It was the last place any of them wanted to be ever again.

"She's in here somewhere guys, we just need to find her and get out." Kane did his best to focus everyone on the job in hand, although he could feel the tension strangling them all from the moment they'd walked in.

JJ's light struck the door first as they approached it.

The weathered brass number 6 glimmered innocently as the petrified group gathered around it, waiting for someone to pluck up the courage to try the handle.

JJ stepped forward tentatively,"It's locked shut," he said, rattling the door. "What is it with this place? It's done nothing but mess with us since we found it!" JJ was on the verge of losing it. Crooked House was slowly wearing him down, bleeding him dry of his natural zeal.

BANG!
BANG!
BANG!

A loud pounding came from the other side of the door. JJ nearly leapt out of his skin, then breathed a heavy sigh of relief once he realized it was Meridia.

She was crying angry, frustrated tears as she screamed, "I'm in here! The stupid door won't open!"

"It's ok, we're here," JJ replied.

"Get me out of here! Please! I think there's something else still in here with me."

"Step back from the door," JJ warned as he and Kane prepared themselves to break it down.

They both kicked in unison with all their might, but the door didn't budge. There was barely a mark on it by the time they'd both ran out of steam.

"Solid wood..." JJ wheezed, lifting his cap up a little to air his sweaty forehead.

Kane gave the door one more petulant kick in anger.

"Damn it!" he shouted.

A little girl's playful giggle broke out from over his shoulder, echoing all around them.

They were being mocked.

"Let her out!" Zach yelled, his voice close to breaking. Fists clenched in anger; he was picturing how scared Meridia must have been on the other side of the door.

"There might be a key in the office," Izzy muttered, almost to herself.

Kane heard her and immediately started making his way across the living space in the direction of where he thought it was.

"Stay there JJ. Zach, come with me–I'll need you to light the way."

18

The brothers defiantly walked side by side through Crooked House. They were not willing to tolerate any more tricks from the B&B.

Zach illuminated the way, scampering to keep pace with Kane's longer strides. His torch swung from left to right as they made their way through the building. It was much more effective than the light on JJ's camera and showed just how neglected the B&B's interior was.

Sage green wallpaper decorating the hallway had strips missing, exposing cracked plaster underneath. From the corner of his eye, Zach caught an assortment of spiders scuttling away, as if his light had just exposed a secret convention they'd been attending in the shadows. Once they had passed the living space Zach's torch hovered over another bit of graffiti on the door of room 2.

Boldly, in bright white spray-paint were the words *'BURN IN HELL'*.

Zach wondered for a moment what it meant.

Opposite that, in the hall, *'AS BELOW, SO ABOVE'* had crudely been etched into the woodwork with a knife.

Even the most innocuous things he saw took on a wider, more troubling meaning now. He couldn't stop thinking about how scared Meridia must have been. He didn't know how or why she ended up back here. If only he'd been holding her hand when they watched the video footage. Perhaps she wouldn't have vanished, or maybe he would have gone with her.

Kane stopped in his tracks and put an arm across his *'mini-me'*, bringing him to an immediate halt. They had arrived at their destination.

The office was on the opposite side of the building from room 6. It seemed crammed into a tiny corner space between the frosted glass porch with the creepy rocking chair and room 1. It looked like only a cupboard in size; a builder's afterthought. Like all the other rooms in Crooked House, its door was closed when they reached it, however this one was unlocked.

The door let out a soft *creak* as Kane gingerly opened it, and both boys entered cautiously, shielding their mouths from the stale, dusty air they had set free.

"Aargh!" Zach let out a terrified scream and staggered into the room, flailing his arms around and sending his brother into a state of panic.

"What?! What is it?!" Kane barked, tightening his grip on the tennis racket whilst his eyes flitted around the dingy room in search of what was attacking Zach.

"It's a spider! Get it off me!"

"You tit! I nearly shat myself then!" Kane snapped as he dusted his brother's back. "It's only a cobweb...you'll live."

Once he had recovered, Zach scanned the room with his torch.

A small wooden desk was the first thing they noticed on the opposing wall, likely meant to greet guests. The rest of the room was sparse. A lonely bottle-green table lamp sat upright on the desk collecting dust, and a row of gun metal filing cabinets covered the wall to the left of where Kane stood.

The brothers both stepped further into the room, not being fooled by its harmless appearance.

In the background, Meridia had started thumping rhythmically on the door to room 6 again. The sound reverberated down the hall, giving the sinister B&B its own heartbeat. Like an ominous countdown, the sound embodied the strain on everyone, but also jolted the two brothers from their procrastinating in the office doorway.

Having satisfied themselves, the room was empty; Kane located the desk drawers and began rifling through them.

"Shine your torch over here," he barked and then hurriedly emptied the contents of each drawer onto the desktop with a clatter. A pot of half-spent crayons spilled across the glossy wooden surface, as if trying to escape the chaos. "Nothing useful here…"

The second drawer was more fruitful as they both heard the unmistakable sound of keys jangling together when Kane lifted the box. He emptied it under the light of Zach's torch, and their ears hadn't deceived them. A collection of numbered keys sat in the middle of the table.

"Yes!" exclaimed Kane as he victoriously swiped them off the table.

They both rushed toward the exit but stopped suddenly in their tracks.

The door they had come in through only a moment ago, the door they had left open, had completely vanished.

In its place was now a solid white brick wall. Both boys rushed toward the mysterious barricade and began desperately patting it down in search for an opening.

They were trapped.

"There's gotta be an way out," Zach whimpered. "Meridia needs us."

"Fuuuck!!" Kane raged as his temper boiled over. He'd had enough now and began shouting at the ceiling in frustration. "Stop fucking with us! We didn't do anything to you! Let us out!" He shouted himself hoarse as Zach continued to pat and push the wall, looking for a weakness to exploit.

"It's solid. I...I can't move it," he sobbed, slumping against it in defeat.

With that, the childish, eerie giggle erupted once more. The deafening noise came from every corner of the office, forcing Zach and Kane to cover their ears. The laughter persisted with no escape, taunting them repeatedly, like a broken record. Echoing around them.

"Stop!!" Zach shouted in defiance.

The noise subsided, and all they could hear was their own breathing. They both stepped back to get a better look at the problem at hand.

"This can't be real," Kane gasped in exasperation. But the wall felt very real indeed.

"Wait, look!" shouted Zach as he shone his torch at the brickwork.

A black line emerged at the bottom of the wall, as if drawn by invisible charcoal. Zach followed it with his torch as it continued in a straight line towards the ceiling. It stopped halfway up the wall, then after a moment's pause continued moving right at a ninety-degree angle. After traveling a short distance, the line stopped again before finally traveling back down toward the floor.

"It looks like a door," Kane whispered to his wide-eyed brother.

Without another word, Kane stepped toward the outline and gave it a push. The brickwork cracked and creaked under the pressure. White chalk dust peppered Kane's hands as the wall slowly gave way.

"It's working," he declared. "Help me push."

The two boys continued to push until an opening appeared, just like a door as Kane suspected.

Zach directed his torch at the newly formed cavity, void of anything. It was beyond dark, as if nothing even existed on the other side.

"Perhaps it hasn't been drawn yet?" Zach thought to himself as he tried to make sense of what was happening.

He turned his torch on the rest of the office behind them; everything else remained unchanged. There were no other secret passages to be found. The only way they could leave the room and save their friend now was through the mysterious door in front of them.

Zach grabbed Kane's hand and looked at him through eyes of sheer grit and determination.

They exchanged a knowing nod as they both stepped into the unknown.

19

Meridia was terrified now.

She had never suffered from claustrophobia in her life, but here in the dark confines of room 6 she felt as if the walls were closing in on her. Worn out from pounding at the door with clenched fists, she sat dejected on the edge of the bed listening to JJ and Izzy's efforts to reassure her.

They sounded miles away.

The room's chill had made it all the way into her bones now, and she was too exhausted to fight it. There was no bedding to keep her warm. Nothing she could use to break the windows. Meridia sobbed. Her only hope was her friends on the other side of the heavy, seemingly unbreakable door which held her captive.

Outside in the hallway, JJ and Izzy had run out of ideas. Without a key, they were unsure how to free Meridia and stay out of trouble with the police.

"What's taking them so long?" Izzy asked.

"I'm going to find out," JJ replied in resignation. "You stay here and keep talking to Meridia. I'll be back before you know it."

Izzy contemplated her options. As much as she'd always been guided by logic, even her deep-rooted scepticism couldn't formulate a logical reason for whatever was happening here. She mulled over the prospect of being left alone in the hallway, in the dark with God only knew what roaming the building.

She stepped closer to the door of room 6 and in a soft, hushed tone said, "Meridia?... Meridia, it's Izzy. James and I are going to go look for a key. We'll be right back, I promise." She placed her palm flat against the door and paused for a moment as she thought about how scared and alone her best friend was on the other side. "I promise," she reiterated before setting off with JJ to track down the missing Jackson brothers.

The short walk across the living space was tense as they both edged slowly and deliberately to the far corner, led by the dim light coming through the opaque porch door. Their torches moved from side to side, half guiding their way, half trying to flush out any unwanted surprises.

A glass bottle went skating along the floor at speed, crashing into the far wall with an almighty *clink*!

Izzy froze in horror, waiting for the creature to jump out of the shadows.

"Sorry," whispered JJ, "I didn't see it in the dark."

Izzy rolled her eyes as she breathed a deep sigh of relief at JJ's clumsiness. They both stifled a nervous laugh at his expense and then continued to move forward.

As they approached the office door, they saw it was ajar, but there was no sign of any light from Zach's torch.

"Kane?... Zach?..." JJ struggled to find his voice as he called out for his missing friends, trying his best not to draw any unwanted attention. He shone his camera light into the office, hoping to see them both there safe and sound. Alas, the room was empty. The office desk was buried beneath loose crayons, paperclips, and other random items, but nothing there seemed of much use at first glance.

"Kane?... Zach?..." JJ pressed, raising his voice a little.

Nothing.

Izzy's gaze shifted to the filing cabinets as JJ surveyed the items on the desk. She pulled the first drawer to investigate. The sound of metal scraping against metal sliced through the rising pressure in the room and a row of files emerged like a train exiting a tunnel.

Her eyes quickly studied the folder headings in front of her. Izzy was a fast reader so she quickly thumbed through the titles to see if there was something that could provide them with any answers. The uncertainty of it all made her squirm almost as much as the creature in room 6. Her thumb stopped on a file, and she excitedly pulled it out of the cabinet.

"James! Come and look at this!"

20

Kane and Zach first noticed the temperature upon entering the dark chasm. Crooked House felt cold, considering the time of year and the fact it had been left dormant for months, but this place was freezing. The entire atmosphere was icy and intense, assaulting their senses as they entered.

Kane's bones began to ache and seize-up as the air pressure drastically increased, whilst a strange tingling sensation attacked his inner ear like the onset of tinnitus.

"It smells...like fresh...snow..." Kane slurred, but his voice trailed off into the void.

Confused and disorientated, Zach's torch seemed to have no effect on their surroundings. It was as if they were standing in the middle of a black hole.

They took a few steps forward and glanced back at the room behind them. The office they had just come from was getting smaller and smaller, as if they were still travelling away from it, or it was physically shrinking. They tried to run back, but the dimly lit doorway to the office continued to move further and further away and allude them.

Whatever gateway they had just walked through was now closing fast.

"Kane....Zach..." The crackly whisper came from the portal that was rapidly fading in front of them, but it sounded miles away; like a phantom radio frequency their dad sometimes picked up when changing stations in the car.

The last thing either boy saw was JJ entering the office and rushing towards the desk.

"JJ! Over here!.. JJ!..." They tried to call out to him, but it was too late. The door, and the world they had left behind, vanished before their eyes, leaving them engulfed in total darkness.

Zach grasped Kane's shivering hand as he quickly spun around with the torch in search of anything that could help get their bearings. Wherever they were, it seemed to get colder and colder.

An icy wind picked up, and it immediately started to bite. Water streamed down both boys' cheeks as they tried to shield themselves from the elements, which were growing more severe by the second. The arctic wind whistled as it picked up more speed. Its ferocious screeching overpowering any attempts they made to communicate. For a second Zach questioned if he had fallen to his knees, then realized he couldn't feel the ground beneath him anymore. He couldn't feel anything anymore. The bleak conditions had numbed all his senses.

Lost in the abyss, a peculiar ball of white light circled them, growing brighter and faster with each new lap. Neither boy saw where it came from, but it seemed to synchronize with the whistling wind. The brighter the light became, the more intense the whistling. Within seconds, the light was constant and blinding, whilst the whistling was so strong they felt their bodies vibrating under the strain. Then, just as their senses had reached breaking point, everything subsided and faded away.

The sudden release of pressure turned their limbs to jelly.

Zach and Kane slowly opened their eyes, not knowing what to expect. Everything around them was a blur as they struggled to adjust to their new surroundings.

It was daylight, or so they thought, and the warmth of summer gently caressed their skin. They felt a strange crunching underfoot, like dried autumn leaves, as they shuffled around on the spot trying to coax their eyes into cooperating. When they eventually composed themselves, neither boy could believe what they were seeing.

In front of them was a vibrant, life-size crayon drawing of Crooked House, awash with waxy hues of pink and grey. Despite its sketchy nature, the resemblance was unmistakable, including the eerie rocking chair out front. Badly drawn trees framed the lopsided B&B, whilst a series of jagged grey blotches had been strung together to form a path.

Kane traced the path back from the house all the way down to his feet and realized they were both somehow in the picture.

The crunching they felt was, in fact, paper grass, with each blade hand-drawn in vivid green crayon.

"This must be a dream," Kane muttered, as he watched Zach soak up their surreal landscape in wide-eyed bewilderment.

Resembling a cartoon virtual reality, the brothers were the only unchanged elements in the immersive 'picture' they now found themselves in. Aside from the larger-than-life pink house, the only other discernible detail was an impenetrable forest which had been frantically scribbled with thick brown crayon to form a dense prison cell around them.

It reminded Kane of the way he used to rush the backgrounds of all his drawings once he had exhausted colouring in all the interesting bits. *"Definitely the work of a kid,"* he thought to himself. Having surveyed the peculiar landscape and its clear boundaries, the only direction they could take was towards the house.

"I guess we go that way then." He said, gesturing to his brother.

Zach slipped out of his winter coat and tied it firmly around his waist. A lively, yellow scribbled sun flickered in the bright blue sky overhead. Whoever the artist was, this was clearly meant to be a warm summer's day.

As they approached the house, they could see a badly drawn, disproportionate girl in the front window. Again, the detail was sketchy, but it was obviously meant to be Meridia, with her striking red hair and bright blue oversized eyes that were leaking tears. Through the glass porch, they noticed a faint silhouette of another crudely drawn figure.

This time it was the girl they had seen on camera - her yellow dress providing a not-so-subtle clue.

The closer they got to Crooked House, the more detail revealed itself, as if the childish artwork was being rendered in real time. It gave everything the illusion of movement and Kane felt his eyes struggling to adjust under the relentless iterations.

Queasy from motion sickness, they both gingerly lumbered up the path, not knowing where to look. A sharp *click* greeted them as they ascended the wonky steps, and the door opened with a familiar *creak*.

Someone or something was waiting for them.

21

Meridia shuffled herself to the window in the faint hope of a passer-by, but all she saw was row upon row of oppressive trees. Tears raced down her cheeks again as the absence of her friends weighed heavily on her heart.

When they had learned of all the trouble with her dad, Zach and Izzy had really been there for her. They patiently sat through all the tears and tantrums, the heavy-handedness of the courts, and their intrusion on a life they knew nothing about. With them by her side, she felt capable of anything, but this was different. The protective shield they'd helped her build over the last six months had been shattered into tiny pieces, like the dresser mirror that lay scattered over the wooden floor of her prison.

Her mind drifted back to the day's events; that evil creature, the strange 'other' Zach. It was overwhelming. Too much. And now this. *"What monster was lurking in the wardrobe? What if it's out there now, hunting her friends?"* Her imagination shifted gears into overdrive, and she started playing out various scenarios.

None of them ended well.

That was when she saw it.

In the room's darkest corner, she noticed a brief glimmer, as if something shiny had caught the dim light from the window. Squinting her teary eyes, Meridia craned her neck to understand what she was looking at.

Whatever it was, it seemed to be moving.

Click-clack!

Meridia flinched as long talons slowly emerged from the darkness, rapping against the wall before menacingly scraping at the brickwork and leaving a trail of jagged canals in their wake. The sound was excruciating, setting her teeth on edge, as amber brick dust shimmered in the dim light as it gently floated to the ground. A terrifying presence was clawing its way into the room.

Meridia pinched her shoulder blades together to trap the icy chill that was racing up her spine, and that was when the screaming started again.

22

JJ APPEARED OVER IZZY'S SHOULDER AS SHE SHONE HER torch on the folder entitled '*ROOM 6*'.

She opened the file out on top of the extended drawer and began flicking through its contents. In there was a mix of press-cuttings, handwritten notes, and an old photograph; it was a scrap booker's dream and looked to be some kind of fact-file. The first page prominently displayed the little girl from JJ's footage. Someone had written '*Jessica Adams, age 6*' in a black marker pen at the bottom of the photo. '*Missing 20/07/2012*'.

"2012!" JJ gasped in shock.

"Aaargh!!" The ear-splitting scream stopped them both cold in their tracks.

"Meridia," JJ exclaimed.

Izzy scooped up the file, and they both sprinted back to where their friend was being held prisoner. As they approached room 6, the screams became louder and louder, filling them both with dread.

"Where the hell are Zach and Kane? They said they

were going to the office..." Izzy complained as she laboured to keep up with JJ.

"We'll worry about them later, Izz...right now, Meridia needs us. We're coming," he bellowed, darting between the old sofa and armchair to get ahead of Izzy. He arrived at the locked door within seconds and started thumping it with his fist whilst calling out, "Meridia? What's wrong?" The screaming continued relentlessly, oblivious of JJ's arrival.

"MERIDIA!" He shouted again.

"It's here...it's in here with me!" She sobbed.

The shadow creature was forcing its way into Room 6. Shaking and twisting its upper torso erratically, it hissed, and it spat as it tried to vibrate its way through the solid brick wall. Each convulsion was a blur of superhuman speed, followed by a sudden pause as it measured its progress.

Meridia watched in terror as, inch by inch, the monster thrusts its way further and further into the room with her.

Powerless, JJ and Izzy listened to the chaos unfold in room 6, unable to do anything to help their friend.

JJ furiously kicked at the door again in desperation, but it continued to stand firm.

Izzy reopened the folder she'd taken from the office and frantically scanned the contents again in search of something, anything, that could help them.

"Where the hell are Zach and Kane?" she reiterated her annoyance. "They have to be here somewhere."

23

Kane ushered Zach behind him for safety as the porch door opened. It seemed like the inside of the house was still waiting to be drawn, as there was no detail behind it. Instead, they faced yet another pitch-black void.

In the darkness, Kane saw two tiny orbs of light floating towards them.

White knuckled and full of tension, he tightened his grip on his hockey stick and raised it in anticipation, ready to swing at whatever was heading their way.

"Who... who's there?" he asked.

The little girl emerged as she stepped outside into the crayola sunshine. Unlike everything else around them, she seemed very real. Her eyes shimmered as she stared at both boys, and she was covered in ashen dirt like the 'other' Zach. Clutching a tiny retro tin bucket of crayons, she looked solemn as if she'd been crying.

"I can't find my mummy," she sniffled. *"The boogeyman won't let me."*

"What boogeyman?" Zach replied, stepping out from behind his brother.

He'd always had an affinity with younger kids, and as a result, they would often open up to him. His mum always told him it was down to his gentle heart, and that children could sense these things.

"*The boogeyman,*" she continued, "*he won't let me go.*" The girl's voice had an unnatural echo, like it came from the depths of an abandoned well.

"Is that who has our friend?" Zach countered, pointing at the drawing of Meridia at the window.

Electing to stay quiet, Kane watched on as the girl shifted her gaze sheepishly to the ground and shrugged her shoulders.

"*He made me do it,*" she said.

"Who did?"

"*Him,*" she whispered, pointing back at the picture of Meridia.

A new drawing had appeared beside her; a ferocious spectacle of evil menace with razor-sharp teeth, and claws for fingers. It was the monster they had encountered earlier that day.

Both boys felt a spidery chill scuttle up their spines as they locked eyes with the sprawling mess of frenzied black crayon strokes.

As Zach continued the conversation, Kane struggled to tear his eyes away from the monster's morbidly hypnotic gaze. Despite its basic nature, he felt as if the grisly portrait was alive and watching him. Within a matter of seconds, Zach's voice had gently faded into a distant, monotonous hum. The creature's hateful gaze was mesmerizing and surreptitiously severed all connection between Kane's mind and body. Kane didn't mind however, and felt strangely at peace as he became more and more spaced out.

"Kane... Kane!" Zach broke his trance by repeatedly tugging his sleeve. "Earth to Kane..."

"Sorry, I don't know what happened there. I must have zoned out." Kane blinked heavily and shook his head as if to wake himself up. He wondered if the strange artificial heat had gotten to him. "We need to get back to our friends, now."

"This way," whispered the girl as she turned and disappeared back into the darkness from which she came. *"Follow me..."* her ghostly voice echoed from somewhere within.

The brothers had no choice but to follow her inside the aptly crooked sketch.

As soon as they entered, they found themselves in a small, dark, empty room. In contrast to the previous cartoon-like door they had entered, this room seemed real and devoid of any crayon strokes or childish scribble. The thick musty smell of mould hung heavily in the air, stifling their lungs as they took in their surroundings. The boys couldn't make out anything beyond a few feet in front of them because of the impenetrable gloom that now swamped them.

Their hampered exploration came to an abrupt halt as a spotlight suddenly blazed out from somewhere above with a loud *click*.

The sharp contrast of harsh light made both boys jump as it struck an old wooden puppet theatre against the wall in front of them.

Kane felt Zach cling onto his forearm in fright as the dazzling beam clipped the head of a grotesque wooden gargoyle perched on the very top of the theatre. It stared down at them with its beady eyes wearing a wicked smirk on its gnarled face. Kane traced its distorted shadow to the opposite corner of the room where it sat ten times its actual size, glaring at them like a malevolent vulture waiting for the right moment to swoop down on its prey. He felt all the moisture in his mouth evaporate as he tried to console his trembling kid-brother.

"It's...ahem...it's going to be ok mate..."

As Kane continued to scrutinize the ragged theatre looming over them, it transported him back to the Punch and Judy tents he saw at the seaside when he was younger. They always fascinated him with their macabre puppets and violent storylines.

The theatre's exterior was old and rotten. Flakes of chipped blue paintwork clung on to its carcass like flesh on a half-eaten animal. Its stage was hidden behind ragged, grubby red curtains which were drawn together in anticipation of a show waiting to begin.

"This place keeps getting weirder and weirder," Kane quipped as a broken trumpet stomped its way around them, filling the room with its disjointed tune.

The curtains opened jerkily to reveal a dingy stage, and a disturbing string puppet, with a bulbous head made from porcelain, slowly rose from the shadows inside. Wearing a grubby yellow dress, its face was deathly white; punctuated by cavernous eye sockets and bright red-ringed pupils that glowed beneath the spotlight. A demented, toothy grin completed its chilling expression, which was then framed by straggles of lank brown hair sprouting from a hole at the top of its skull.

The very sight of it made Zach shudder. A creepy voice sneered from beneath the theatre's stage,

"Hello everybody... my name is Jesssssickka."

High in pitch, it had a strange hiss-like quality to it, the way snakes often sounded in cartoons. The creepy attempt at mimicking a little girl's voice made Kane's skin crawl, and he instantly began conjuring up ominous images of its source.

Whatever it was behind all this, he'd seen enough horror movies in his time to realize they weren't safe here.

Something sinister was hiding right in front of them.

24

Meridia stopped screaming.

Her voice was hoarse now and her ruckus wasn't helping matters. She cuffed her tears away so she could see clearly.

The creature was more than half-way free from the restrictions of the wall, and she guessed she only had a matter of minutes left to live. Its bald head jerked abruptly, like a bird sizing up its prey, while its searing eyes never strayed from Meridia. When still, its skin was a translucent blur, like a patchwork of shadows, but its teeth and claws looked razor-sharp and deadly. Cloaked in a tattered black robe, the monster defied gravity as it wiggled and wormed its way into the room, ebbing and flowing as if underwater. Each movement the creature made fanned the room with a warm smell of decaying rot, choking Meridia as she sat paralyzed with fear, trying desperately to avoid making eye-contact. Its luminous pupils were mesmerizing, but she had to stay sharp and alert if she was ever going to make it out of the room alive.

Out in the hallway, JJ had taken his cap off and pressed

his forehead against the door in defeat when he suddenly had an epiphany. He picked up his cricket bat and grabbed Izzy by the hand.

"Come with me," he insisted. "We need to go back outside."

Izzy got up off the floor and pulled the file back together for the second time, tucking it under her arm.

JJ then whispered through the door, "Meridia...Meridia, we're going outside to break the window. Stay as far away as you can. We're getting you out now."

At the news of JJ's plan, Izzy kicked herself for not thinking of this sooner. Swept up in blind panic, they had all been so focused on what was going on inside the house, none of them had considered breaking her out from there. They both raced down the grungy hallway and out of the house the same way they had entered. It was noticeably darker outside now as the evening approached.

When they reached the correct window, JJ cupped his hands around his face and peered through the dirty glass. Meridia did what he asked and stood in the opposite corner with her back to the door. Her eyes were fixed on the wall to her right in absolute terror, but JJ couldn't see what she was staring at from his position.

Izzy stood well back as JJ wound the cricket bat far behind his head as if he were about to hit a home run.

He let fly with all his might and the corner of the bat connected perfectly with the centre of the windowpane, sending a shattering *crack* echoing through the cramped room as it smashed into tiny pieces. Using the bat to clear out any jagged shards of glass left in the frame, JJ made sure it was safe for Meridia to climb out.

"Ok, get out now!" he bellowed into the room. He stretched out both arms through the broken window and waved his hands in encouragement for Meridia to make her move.

In the opposite corner, the terrifying creature had now made its way into the room.

The creature, no longer vibrating erratically, was crouched on all fours like a wild animal poised to attack. Razor-sharp nails *clinked* against the hard floor as it steadied itself, all the while staring at its prey.

If Meridia were to make it out, she would need to get across the bed in front of her and out of the window somehow before the monster reached her. The odds were not stacked in her favour as the monster had less distance to travel and looked fast.

The shadowy figure stood upright to a cacophony of bones cracking and towered above everything in the room. It seemed so much larger now, as if it had doubled in size.

Growling and hissing, it arched its back in readiness to leap when a brick came hurtling into the room in its direction.

JJ's intention was to distract the creature, buying Meridia time. The brick passed straight through the monster's cloak as if it wasn't there, striking the wall behind it with a dull *thud* and clattering to the ground.

It was now or never.

Momentarily free from the monster's chilling gaze, Meridia sprinted across the bed and over toward the window ledge. The spongy springs underfoot threatened to topple her over, and it felt as if she was running across one of her mum's jelly trifles. JJ's outstretched arms were waiting for her on the other side, willing her to get to him. As soon as she grabbed onto the ledge, a sharp shooting pain rocketed from her wounded hand all the way up her arm, and she buckled at the elbow. Her escape was academic now though, as JJ gave a huge heave and pulled her through onto the soft marshy grass on the other side. She landed in a heap on top of him while Izzy looked on anxiously.

Meridia was out.

Inside room 6 the creature continued to hiss, but it wasn't hot on Meridia's heels as they'd all expected.

JJ got to his feet, ready for a fight and cautiously peered over the windowsill, half expecting to come face-to-face with the monster. He sighed in relief at the sight of the empty, trampled bed. Once again, the monster had decided not to take up chase. JJ tilted his head a little to see further into the room and saw it stopped just short of the bed. It looked as if it was afraid of the sunlight which was streaming through the broken window, perforating the darkness.

The monster was in a full-blown rage now, slashing and scratching at the air in angst with its lethal claws. In all its fury a claw glanced at the beam of daylight holding it at bay and the creature let out a blood-curdling scream. Its finger emitted a thin fountain of smoke as it retreated to the shadows.

Transfixed, JJ observed the figure dissolve into the darkness like a dusky ghost.

The room was silent and empty once again.

The monster disappeared.

"It's gone," he declared, dumbstruck. "You guys wait here. I'm going back in to find Kane and Zach so we can all get out of this bloody place."

25

Kane surveyed the room. There was no obvious way out.

A solid white brick wall had magically replaced the door they had entered through, just like the one they had seen in the office. They were trapped with the mysterious puppet master.

Kane ushered Zach behind him once again, just a little so as not to freak him out. The only option they had was to keep as much distance as possible between themselves and the dilapidated theatre whilst they let its ominous show play out.

On stage, a taller, equally disturbing, puppet brushed past the shabby curtains and bounced its way into the spotlight next to Jessica. This one was made up like an old Aunt Sally doll, with bright red lips and baby-blue mascara dripping down its cheeks. Its jet-black hair was more voluminous than Jessica's and had been hacked in the shape of a bob which rested just above its mad, staring eyes. Bobbing up and down as if walking in zero gravity, it had a tiny yellow plastic suitcase stapled to its arm, which clattered and rattled as it made its way across the stage.

"*We're gooooing on an advennnnnture,*" came the eerie, disjointed voice as it hypnotically waved the new puppet from side to side in time with each word.

Kane squirmed; unable to peel his eyes from what was unfolding. The voice sounded more unsettling this time, almost slurring, as if the puppet master forced each word out.

"*Okaaaaaay mummmmy,*" Jessica replied, and with an emphatic snap, a canvas rolled down behind both puppets. Replacing the pitch-black backdrop was another crayon drawing of Crooked House.

Zach pointed and whispered to his brother, "Look at the window."

There, next to the front door, was the same badly drawn shadow monster they'd seen earlier. Both puppets merrily bobbed up and down toward the house, oblivious of the sketchy creature staring at them. Then, just as they reached the porch door, the spotlight cut out without warning, plunging everything into total darkness.

Kane went rigid with fear and felt the colour drain from his face. His panic overflowed onto Zach and they gripped onto each other, bracing themselves for something awful to happen. The seconds felt like hours as they blindly clung onto each other for dear life. Before either of them could speak, the spotlight returned with a loud *click*, causing both boys to jump out of their skin.

The second act was about to begin, and both Jessica and her mother were now inside Crooked House.

Long shadows stretched across the tatty canvas, eclipsing the crayon illustration of an office. In the centre of the painted backdrop was a man sat behind the desk Kane had ransacked moments ago. Another chilling, toothy smile was plastered across its face, whilst its deranged eyes, emphasized by thick red circles, stared gormlessly into space. Jessica's mum swayed from side to side as if chatting with the creepy receptionist.

"*Blah blah blah,*" the puppet master croakily narrated. Its jagged, growling voice cut through the silence like a serrated knife. "*Blah... blah... blah.*"

There was something childish about the show.

Underneath the unsettling façade, it was beyond basic, like watching a toddler act out with their favourite toys. Whilst her mother was busy talking, Jessica took her chance.

In true pantomime fashion, the little puppet glanced from side to side and slowly crept away from her mother. The background moved in response, rolling past the living space and onto a row of shoddily numbered rooms and her mother exited stage right. Jessica stopped abruptly outside the door marked '6' and checked if the coast was clear.

The door *clicked* open by itself.

"*Jesssssicaaaaa......Jesssssicaaaaa....*" This time the voice sounded smooth and melodic as it tried its best to lure her inside.

Jessica slowly made her way closer to the door, took one more cursory look behind her, and then slipped inside.

BANG!

The door on stage slammed shut, causing a resounding echo.

The sudden racket made the brothers jump in unison again. Kane tutted shaking his head; he was mad at himself for letting such an insipid jump-scare rattle him. When he returned his attention back to the show, they were already inside room 6.

Once again, the backdrop was faithful to what they'd seen during their first visit to Crooked House.

Jessica was alone in the darkened room and the only prop, which wasn't two dimensional, was a double wardrobe made from oak.

The miniature casket spun, like a magician's cabinet. When it had reached a full rotation, the door opened, and Jessica entered.

For a moment, it looked like she was resisting and being forced into the tiny box against her will. A chorus of mock-gasps rang out as the background faded to black, and the wardrobe door closed, trapping her inside. Then, from behind the tattered curtains, a magic wand appeared and tapped the side of the wardrobe 3 times.

"*Abra Kadabraaaaa*," the strange voice crackled, as the door to the wardrobe *creaked* open to reveal nothing but empty space inside.

Jessica had vanished.

Canned applause broke out around the room, deafening Kane and Zach before stopping abruptly as the show continued its story.

"*Jesssssicaaa?....Jesssssicaa?*" Her mother cried; arms raised as she trembled from left to right in a state of panic. Her oversized mouth was now downturned to the extreme like the tragedy mask at an amateur dramatics club.

As she continued to wail, a puppet dressed as a police officer joined her on stage.

This one was far more conventional as puppets went. Its masculine face sported rosy cheeks and a large protruding chin which poked out from under its police hat.

"Jesssssicaaa?... Jesssssicaaaaaa?" The policeman's tone was much deeper.

"This is Jessica's story," Zach whispered to his brother. "She disappeared right here, in Crooked House. This place is evil!"

"Quiet boooy! Thisss is my stooory!" The puppet master snapped back at Zach's remark, and then petulantly hurled both puppets out of the theatre in his direction. Their fragile, porcelain skulls cracked like hard-boiled eggs as they struck the wooden ground.

The brothers reeled back in shock as both mother and policeman lay staring up at them like a creepy Humpty Dumpty tribute act; their cracked faces now wearing maniacal grins that stretched from ear to ear.

Down amongst the shadows, Zach thought he saw the puppets breathing as their tiny chests began rhythmically expanding and contracting.

"Look," he mumbled to Kane, pointing at the macabre husks at his feet. "They're alive."

Aghast, both brothers watched on in terror as dozens of cockroaches poured out through the gaping cavities where the puppet's foreheads had once been.

"Argh!" Zach screamed, as the swarm of slimy roaches made a beeline for his feet.

Stamp! Crack! Crunch!

The boys furiously stomped on their newfound admirers like they were making wine, only this wine was of the putrid, pus-filled variety. Sticky entrails glued their shoes to the ground as the awful stench of squashed bugs filled the air, stinging their nostrils with its musty aroma.

Zach could taste his own vomit in the back of his throat as he fought to keep his lunch down. Drenched in a cold sweat, he was sure he'd crushed them all now, but continued to trample everything in sight just to be certain.

When the chaos eventually subsided, Kane glanced back up towards the theatre, conscious he'd lost sight of their menacing host.

The wardrobe in room 6 was centre stage again and the puppet master was going through the motions with the same routine as before. Reaching its conclusion, he tapped the wooden prop once more with his wand and triggered a deafening drum roll from somewhere above them.

The door *clicked* open, and as if by magic, Jessica re-emerged.

Her waxen ceramic face was now solemn and her body shaking violently in fear.

A malevolent *"Ta daaaaa,"* bellowed out of the wooden theatre, and the trembling Jessica took a forced bow.

Uncomfortable silence blanketed the room and Kane noticed every anxious fidget his brother was making behind him.

On stage, Jessica sobbed uncontrollably. Jets of inky liquid sprayed outwards from the puppet's button-eyes, soaking both brothers with mock tears.

Despite the abstract and ghoulish nature of the show, Jessica's ordeal, and her sorrow, still felt very real. Whatever dark forces were at play here in Crooked House, they had clearly snatched Jessica away from her mother.

Before they could speak, a strange crackling sound emanated from the theatre, like the static build up on an old vinyl record player. It was faint at first, and barely noticeable.

Kane strained his ears to hear it as he scrutinized the puppet theatre, squinting to overcome the darkness surrounding them.

Its decrepit wooden panels appeared to be moving. He looked closer still as the crackling imposed itself on the room, getting louder and louder. The theatre was expanding and contracting, as if it were breathing. It wobbled and lifted slightly off the ground as the wood began to buckle and splinter.

It wasn't breathing at all.

Something inside was forcing its way out.

26

JJ tip-toed down the hallway of Crooked House, wishing he'd never had his 'wicked idea'. His dad had always told him '*What ifs are just phantom thoughts*', but today had been so extreme he was sure he'd be forgiven for his misgivings.

He figured the best place to start his search would be the office again. Tightening his grip on his trusty cricket bat and raised it next to his head like a samurai, ready to swing at anything with spooky eyes and sharp teeth.

The office door was closed when he got there, causing him to pause. He was certain they left it open when they heard Meridia's screams.

"Kane?... Zach?..." he called softly, in the hope they would answer, but there was no sign of anyone in the dark, dingy hall.

JJ gingerly reached for the door handle when he felt a hand grab his shoulder. His legs wobbled as if he'd been switched off at the mains, but before he could lash out, he heard Meridia's voice.

"It's ok, it's just us," JJ turned and saw Izzy and Meridia standing behind him.

"We weren't going to let you do this on your own, James," Izzy added.

JJ, buoyed by their show of support, turned the office door handle and they all filtered into the room.

Izzy yearned to pick up where she left off at the filing cabinet. Her gut was telling her it held answers, or at the very least, some clues about whatever was going on at Crooked House. Whilst JJ and Merida sifted through the objects on the desk, she grabbed the remaining nine files out of the drawer and placed them on the floor with the one she'd taken earlier. She opened the file marked '*Room 6*' again and started methodically going through each item inside. Meanwhile, Meridia was nervously wittering on about everything she'd experienced since disappearing at Zach's house.

"She knew my name...how did she know my name? One minute I was there...in Kane's room with all of you... and the next...she came out of the tv...like one minute she was on the screen and the next she was towering over me. Her mouth... it opened so wide it was like a cave...I could feel myself leaning into it...like I didn't have a choice. Everything went black and I'm not sure if I closed my eyes or she swallowed me...she was so big by then...filling the room. I wanted to scream...I wanted to run and warn you all, but you couldn't see her...and I couldn't speak...I couldn't move. I sat there like an idiot waiting for her to take me...to bring me back to this place...to the boogeyman..." It all sounded so far-fetched as she said it aloud, but JJ and Izzy were oblivious as they continued to rummage through the files.

"There must be a connection between the girl in the

video, Jessica, and whatever that was in room 6," Izzy put forward. "This file is all about the girl." She had everyone's attention now.

"It says Jessica vanished in 2012 when she was 6 years old. The police searched, but she wasn't found. No witnesses. No suspects. She...vanished...like Jonathan Ashfield."

"So why is she in a folder called room 6?" JJ asked.

"It doesn't say here, I'm going by the newspaper clipping from when she went missing. There are some handwritten notes too, but it's too dark in here to make them out."

"She brought me to room 6," Meridia chimed in. "Maybe she was trying to tell us something?"

"Maybe she was just trying to feed you to that monster," JJ countered.

Meridia mulled over JJ's throwaway remark and wondered if there was any truth in it. Her head was pounding from her ordeal and any attempt to make sense of it all made the pain worse. She was too tired to look for answers and wanted to find the boys so she could go home. As it often did, her mind wandered. The warm embrace of her marshmallow duvet made her forget all her worries, while the soothing amber nightlight on her bedside table gently massaged her weary, bloodshot eyes.

"This doesn't make sense..." Izzy interrupted Meridia's daydream and brought her back to the dingy office with a bump. "This clipping says Jessica went missing in 2012 when she was 6, right?" She held the newspaper cut-out up like a lawyer presenting their case to a jury.

"But the date stamp on this other picture of her here is 2011, and she looks exactly the same as she did in your video, James." Izzy held up her next piece of evidence for everyone to see. It seemed like a still from another video camera, but the resolution was lower than JJ's. However, it was clearly the same girl.

What was more baffling to the group was she appeared to be standing by the window of room 6 when the B&B was still open for business.

"I don't understand," said JJ, more than a little confused, "if she was 6 when she went missing that would make her older than me now, but she still looks like a little kid."

"Plus, she's wearing the same clothes in both photos," Meridia added. "What if she's the one haunting this place and wants us to free her? That's what always happens in ghost films, isn't it? Maybe her remains are in there somewhere..." her imagination was taking over again.

"Let's think about this logically," Izzy interjected. "We've now seen two pictures of the same girl taken 12 years apart. She looks the same in both and is even wearing the same clothes. Her eyes look black in our picture, but I'm unsure about this older one. She kidnapped Meridia somehow from Kane's bedroom and brought her here to room 6. Let's say you're right and she is a ghost. She either brought you to room 6 because that's where she disappeared, or she wanted to feed you to that monster like James said." Izzy was pacing now, and her synapses were threatening to overheat.

"We also know someone was keeping a file on her and that room before she even went missing. Can ghosts time travel? Or did the person who took that picture have something to do with her disappearance? There are files for every room here, and each one looks like it's about a different person. Some are full, like Jessica's, and others have next to nothing in them. So, does that mean there are other ghosts here? And who was keeping the files in the first place? The missing owner?... Who am I kidding? I'm trying to look at this logically, but none of this is logical at all." Izzy was wrestling back tears now and losing.

Merida wrapped her arms around her, like a big sister, and Izzy's hypothesizing descended into a gentle sob muffled by Meridia's shoulder.

"We need to search the rest of this place now," JJ bleated. With limited daylight left, they didn't want to be in Crooked House at night. It was time for him to step up. "We need to search every room if we have to. They must be here somewhere."

27

Kane and Zach looked on in horror as the puppet theatre continued to crack and break apart from the inside. They were in real trouble now and there wasn't anywhere to run.

Desperate to escape, both boys frantically searched the room for a way out as props from the creepy show crashed and clattered to the ground around them.

The floor was littered with darkly comedic props and cracked cockroach shells. Crayons rolled towards them and unused backgrounds full of murder and mayhem floated to the ground like feathers. The theatre shook high above them now and was almost scraping the ceiling.

Whatever was in there was big.

Bigger than any human could be.

With a final push, the wooden box exploded apart, and they came face to face with the creature inside it. It looked like the monster they had encountered in room 6, this one towered way above them and must have been close to eight feet tall.

Its face was gaunt, with the same soft-focus skin made

from shadows. Its eyes were deep-set but sparkled in the dark like stars. Filling the room with its contorted body, a cackling laughter erupted from its gaping mouth that sounded as if it had escaped from the depths of hell.

In its long, thin, razor-sharp claws it held Jessica's puppet by her legs.

She appeared to be wriggling, as if alive and trying to break free from the monster's clutches.

In the chaos Kane swore he heard the tiny puppet scream in fear as the creature raised her high above its head and opened its mouth wider in anticipation. The glistening claws released their grip and sent the tiny effigy tumbling through the air. It fell to its end, through the jagged gates of the creature's mouth, and was swallowed whole.

"Weeee've beeeeen waiting for you Zacccchh!" the creature declared. Its voice was incohesive and grim. Brilliant eyes, as bright as the moon, bore down on the brothers who now had their backs firmly pressed against the wall behind them.

"Don't look at its eyes," in the thick of the commotion, each brother assumed this advice had come from the other.

'There must be a way out,' thought Kane as he held his hockey stick in a readiness for a fight.

"The crayon..." The voice came again, this time right next to Zach's ear.

Whilst Kane prepared himself to do battle with their captor, Zach turned to face the white brick wall.

He glanced down at a bright yellow crayon that had landed at his feet, stuck in slimy roach mucus, and forced himself to pick it up.

The monster glided closer and closer while Zach shakily drew a door on the wall behind them.

A lightbulb illuminated in Kane's brain as he saw what his brother was doing and made the connection.

As soon as Zach reached the floor with his final stroke, Kane shoulder-barged the rectangular shape in front of them. The idea was sound, and the door cracked open for both boys to scramble through. On the other side was a long dark corridor with a faint light of hope at the opposite end.

It was too far for either of them to see what was creating it, but they had no choice but to keep moving in case the monster followed them. They sprinted, Kane ensuring that he stayed behind his brother for protection. Frantic footsteps echoed on the ground as they traversed the narrow passageway, urged onward by the monster's sinister laugh cackling after them.

"There's noooo escaaaape!" Came the booming, raucous voice behind them.

Warm breath brushed the back of Kane's neck as he tried to hurry Zach along, but the exit didn't seem to get any closer. Enormous cracks violently zig-zagged along the walls, overtaking them both as plaster fell ahead. They felt caught in an earthquake.

Kane couldn't risk looking back in case he stumbled, so he launched his hockey stick behind him in the hope it might buy more time. Up ahead he could hear his brother sobbing, but they had to keep going.

The light ahead was closer now and through tears Zach could make out the green table lamp they'd seen in the office. It was switched on and guiding them back home. Debris continued to cascade from the ceiling up ahead, but they narrowly side-stepped it.

They had made it to the final stretch.

"Run!" came the friendly voice again, echoing around them. *"It's coming!"*

28

That was the last thing they heard as they both entered the office with a bang, crashing into the desk and knocking it onto its back.

JJ had hardly made it out of the office door when he heard the kerfuffle behind him. The brothers leapt up from the crumpled heap they'd landed in and charged toward him, screaming.

A huge, ominous shadow skulked across the room and enveloped the upturned desk as the creature burst onto the scene seconds behind them. Its tattered, translucent robe moved like tentacles, gripping the walls to help it pivot in the direction of the fleeing children. It bounded after them on all fours like a wild animal, hissing through clenched teeth that resembled broken glass.

First the brothers swept up JJ, then Izzy, and finally Meridia, in a surge of hysteria, trying to break out of their diabolical confines.

Pouring out into the living space, JJ could hear the monster's claws scraping on the stone floor as it galloped behind them. There was no way they would all outrun it.

He side-stepped from the crowd, letting Kane and Zach overtake him.

When they were clear, he stepped back into the path of the oncoming creature and swung his cricket bat as hard as he could in its direction. The blow connected with the creature, glancing the side of its head just as it was rushing forward. The strike felt odd to JJ, as if he'd just hit a balloon. For a millisecond he thought he had missed his target altogether, but the creature was sent sprawling way off-course into the yellow sofa. It must have been as light as a feather, JJ thought to himself as he turned to re-join the race to escape.

He saw the others had reached the final hallway and would make it to the door now.

That was when JJ froze.

A strange force spun him around, pushing him to the ground on his back.

"Oof!" The bone-crunching fall knocked all the wind right out of him, leaving him dazed and wheezing on the ground. It was as if the creature hadn't laid a finger on him, and more like the surrounding air had conspired to bring him down.

As he lay there stunned and unable to catch his breath, the monster loomed over him, the way a triumphant cat would over a mouse.

"JJ! NO!" Kane's cry of desperation stopped everyone else in their tracks.

"Leave him alone!" Izzy screamed, her voice breaking as tears began streaming out from under her glasses.

Spluttering and panicking, JJ held his cricket bat at each end and pushed it out in front of him to fend the creature off. It weighed nothing, yet it was too strong for him to hold at bay. The cricket bat edged closer and closer to his own throat, as if the monster were toying with him.

With enticing eyes, it had a twisted sneer on its face as it glared down at him.

JJ felt his body weaken, as if he was falling asleep. All he could do was stare deep into the eyes in front of him. He found himself transfixed and, although he vaguely sensed everything happening around him, he didn't seem to care when his body started to go numb.

29

Meridia had reached her limit. Her cheeks were flushed and her eyes ablaze as she charged as fast as her tired legs would carry her back down the hallway and in the direction of JJ.

The huge shadowy mass swamped and suffocated the narrow corridor. Somewhere underneath, JJ was in grave danger.

When she arrived, all she thought to do was jump on the monster's back. All she needed to do was distract it long enough for JJ to break free. She threw her arms around the creature's neck and heaved backwards with all her weight. It felt like she was wrestling with the wind as her hands tried to grip and pull at the beast's neck.

She felt it snapping and cracking under her; the way dried autumn leaves break underfoot.

The creature's head turned around to face her, jarring and jolting as if it was forcing its body to contort against its own nature. Its arms followed suit, as elbows bent back and wrists twisted and turned their attention away from JJ and towards her.

Meridia's reflection was aghast, captured by the black glassy eyes that were now locked with hers.

She couldn't look away.

They were so close to her now she could feel the monster's stale, rancid breath on her lips. A slight breeze lifted her hair as Kane brushed past them both at speed.

He tried desperately to pull the monster away from his friends. Zach and Izzy then entered the fray, and all began kicking and pulling at the monster in different directions.

"*Enooouuuugh!*" the monster roared as it twisted its entire body like a corkscrew in the air, shrugging off Meridia and Kane as if they were both rag dolls. The creature gracefully landed on whatever it had for feet under its robes and found itself dividing the group.

Izzy, Meridia and a motionless JJ lay sprawled across the floor on one side of it, whilst on the other, Kane was already back on his feet and shielding his brother anticipating the next attack.

"What do you want?!" Kane demanded in defiance. "Leave us alone!"

"*It was yoooou that came heeeeeere.*"

"We're sorry, ok? Just let us go and we won't come back!"

"*Yoooou were alllllwaaays meant to come. Weeeee've been waiting...*"

During the exchange, Meridia and Izzy shook JJ to wake him up, never taking their eyes off the back of the towering creature in front of them.

Izzy noticed light pouring in through the opaque glass door of the porch behind them.

The sun was setting.

They needed to get out of Crooked House before it disappeared completely.

"Just let us go, please..." Zach pleaded. He was sobbing again and couldn't see a way out unless the monster allowed them.

On the other side of their sinister adversary, JJ sat up with a start.

"The light..." came the voice, shouting right in his ear *"use the light..."*

JJ glanced behind and saw the monster now closing in on Zach and Kane, its claws were outstretched at either side blocking any way past. Half dazed from his ordeal; JJ fumbled around on the ground next to him in search of his cricket bat. He discovered it under one of the old magazines that had been scattered during the struggle.

He snatched at the handle.

Clumsily getting back to his feet, he staggered towards the porch door and hit the glass pane dead centre with all the energy he had left. Half of the pane broke and shattered on the porch outside.

A huge beam of beautiful, unfiltered daylight poured into the room, racing up the hall and hitting the monster square on the back.

An ear-splitting, harrowing scream exploded from the creature's mouth in response as the light seemed to pierce its body like a laser beam. Arching its back as it recoiled from the pain, the brilliant white light burst through the creature's chest, blinding Kane and Zach. It seemed rooted to the spot now, impaled on the shaft of light and screaming in agony.

As the monster flailed its arms in frustration, clawing at the lucent air surrounding it, JJ ruthlessly swung at the remaining shards of glass, allowing more daylight to stream in.

Another beam struck the creature, then another, then

another, as each new swing from JJ's bat inflicted more pain. A choking, acidic mist filled the air, encircling the monster like a tornado. It spun faster and faster as the light travelled with it, dazzling everyone in its wake. The scream became distorted, like static on the radio, until the light filled the entire hall. It felt like they were all trapped inside a vacuum, being pulled towards the intense spinning light. Deafened and blinded by what was happening, the building shook around them as they clung on to whatever they could. They were at the very limit of what they could endure now as invisible forces threatened to tear them apart.

Meridia's screaming replaced the sound of the creature's as the light faded and the pressure subsided until the house was once again still. JJ lowered his arm that had been shielding his eyes to find the monster had vanished.

"It's gone," he declared. "The light...I think the light must've killed it!" with that Meridia stopped her screaming and dropped to one knee in search of her breath.

"We need to get out of here now!" Kane barked and ushered everyone towards him. They didn't need two attempts to find their way out of Crooked House this time. Drenched in sweat and exhausted, Kane held the loose panel open for everyone to get out.

Izzy scooped up the files that were now littered in the hallway as she made her way to the exit.

They all limped, tripped, and staggered onto the grass outside. The frigid evening air burnt Zach's lungs as he crouched on all fours, sobbing.

"We need to keep moving," Kane gasped; his voice was hoarse now. He had to get everyone up off the ground and as far away from Crooked House as possible.

There was an eerie silence outside the B&B, and Kane wondered if this was just the calm before another storm.

He'd seen enough horror movies in his time to know there is always a false dawn before the real finale and recognized there was a chance the monster might jump out on them one last time.

He didn't want to stick around to find out either way.

Day was passing its baton to night, and they still needed to make their way back home. Despite how terrified they were, none of the group had the energy to run this time. They were all dog-tired and so backed away from the B&B in fear of any more ghastly surprises it held for them.

30

Inside Crooked House, its halls were still.

There was no haunting laughter or lost little girls roaming the corridors. The guest in room 4 watched from the shadows as all five children headed towards the woods.

Oh, how he would *"love to hunt them down right now,"* he thought to himself. What fun it would be to hear their screams echo amongst the trees.

Their time would come, though.

He was promised he could kill them once his masters had claimed the runt of the litter; a boy named Zach.

It was already decided, just like his fate had been. His palms itched at the thought of wielding his knife again in the crisp night air. Despite his thirst for blood, he remained patient.

He could wait.

He had all the time in the world…

31

Izzy gripped the files close to her chest like a comfort blanket as she trudged through the woods. Her mind was racing as she struggled to reconcile anything she'd seen today. There was no explanation for any of it, and she was just as frightened by that as she was by the monsters of Crooked House.

She had grown up in a house that valued science and logic above all else, and in just a few hours, her entire world had been completely upended. Her only hope of answers lay in the files she clung onto so desperately and she planned to find them once she had got some much-needed sleep.

Leaden legs battled with the bumpy terrain as a grimace crept over her face, almost pushing her glasses off. She was sure she'd seen enough to haunt her dreams for a lifetime and wondered if she would ever sleep again. She leaked a caring glance at Zach, who had been steadily sobbing since they'd escaped.

He walked with his head down and eyes firmly fixed on the ground. His wavy mop of hair was ruffled forward to hide his tears from the others. He looked completely broken.

"It's going to be ok Zach," Izzy tried to reassure. She wasn't good at comforting boys or girls for that matter.

Zach glanced up at her and cuffed his tears away.

"What if it comes back for me?" he sniffled. "They took Meridia in front of us, and we didn't even see it happen. What if...what if they take me tonight when I'm in bed?" He shivered as his body succumbed to the late afternoon chill.

All he could do was replay the monster's words in his head. He had no idea why they had picked him, or how they even knew his name. He hoped JJ was right, and the sunlight had killed it, but something niggling within him said this wasn't over. For a start, there was the other creature they'd seen in room 6. *Where did that go*, he wondered. All he knew for sure was Crooked House was no ordinary haunting. Whatever terrors lurked within its walls were very real, and very dangerous.

"We won't let that happen," Meridia chimed in. "None of us are going to let that happen. It's over. The monster is dead, and we're never going back to that place ever again." She was still quietly seething.

Meridia wore her heart on her sleeve and had quite the temper when she was pushed too far.

Crooked House had pushed her way beyond all her limits.

She petulantly kicked at the fallen twigs as she marched through the woods. The crisp chill in the air did nothing to cool her bright red cheeks that were flush with indignation. Her anger had distracted her from how scared she was, like a defence mechanism. Zach was right though, and she knew only too well how easy it was to be watching tv one minute and locked in a room with a monster the next.

She booted a sizeable branch and paused for a moment to pick it up. It was heavy and the rough bark felt uncomfortable in her hand. *'It's heavy though'*, she told herself and decided it would serve her well as a weapon until she reached home.

She looked at Kane and JJ, who chatted up ahead. Meridia wondered if she knew all there was to know about today's terrifying events. She'd been locked in that room for what felt like an eternity. All she could see with each heavy blink were those black, shiny eyes staring back at her from the shadows.

"What do we do now?" JJ asked. He still had brain fog from his trance and his head was banging like a drum.

Despite his heroics, he was acting on pure instincts when he smashed the glass door, and the whole thing was a bit of a blur. He still had no clue who had told him to break the window. It felt as if it had come to him in a dream, or a vision. He remembered once reading about people hearing voices when they needed them most and shook his head, still perplexed. Whatever it was, it had saved their lives today.

"We need to come up with a plan," Kane stepped over JJ's thoughts. "We can't tell anyone else; they'll think we're mad. And that includes the police cos we had no right being there in the first place. Even the footage we bagged earlier looks like a prank. Found footage posts are ten-a-penny on YouTube and have been ever since The Blair Witch."

JJ nodded lethargically in agreement as they approached the roadside. A blanket of calm covered the five friends as they heard the familiar sound of cars whizzing past on the main road.

"Civilization," Meridia sighed from behind them.

It was almost dusk now, and they all heard the *clanking* of the gates to Jubilee Park being locked by the warden as they approached.

"I think we should all go back to ours for pizza," Kane proposed. "Our dad left us some money for dinner, and we need to make sure everyone's ok before they go home." Pizza sounded appealing to everyone right now. They were all exhausted, frozen, and starving.

"Sounds good," JJ said. He was never one to turn down free food, especially pizza.

32

The Jackson house always felt welcoming, which is why the group had adopted it as their second home over the years.

Warm mahogany featured throughout, perfectly paired with ochre-coloured lampshades that combined to create a relaxed and cozy ambience. The informal soft seating reinforced the house was built for comfort and despite having all the mod cons one could hope for, it never felt too showy. Instead, it proudly displayed its scuffed woodwork and frayed cushions, wearing them like badges of honour to create a well-worn and lived-in setting.

Maybe it was the sudden rush of sugar from the Pepsi they'd all gulped down, or the signature aroma of freshly baked cakes drifting in from the kitchen that had put them all at ease, but everyone perked up a little as they huddled round Kane's dining table. A chaotic hubbub had replaced the reflective silence on their walk back as everyone emptied their stories all at once.

"Guys! Guys! Let's all calm down for a minute." Kane interjected above the noise. "The pizza will be here soon, and we won't hear the door at this rate," he stood up and got everyone's attention.

He held a pen and pad in his hand that he'd fetched from his room.

"Let's go round the table and capture everything that happened. We all got separated at different times today, so we need to make sure we get everything down while it's fresh in our heads." Kane had seen a detective follow this process in one of the '*It's Behind You*' movies, and it had helped catch the killer.

They needed to capture every detail if they were ever going to make sense of today's events.

"I don't know if we'll ever make sense of what happened today..." JJ added, rubbing his temples. "I know we've seen a lot of horror films over the years, mate, but I've not seen half of what was in that place today. I mean...what was that thing in the shadows? That was no ordinary ghost...if there is such a thing. The creepy little girl...now that I can believe was a ghost...but razor-sharp teeth and claws trying to throttle me to death is a whole different bag."

"You should've seen the fucked-up puppet show it put on before it chased us out of the office...and the weird cartoon drawing we got sucked into! It was like a twisted version of Mary Poppins." Kane's throwaway comment drove home the inconceivable nature of what they'd all witnessed.

"The one I was trapped with was different...it was more like a wild animal...like the first one we saw..." Meridia couldn't bring herself to use the word 'monster' in her description. That would mean letting the boogeyman into her world, and once that happened, there would be no going back.

"Kane's right guys...we need to get all this stuff down

while it's fresh. I may not have been kidnapped by a ghost or held prisoner in a drawing, but I've seen enough to know that place is more than just a haunted house." Izzy had a steely look as she peered over her glasses at everyone around her.

"Let's get to it then..." Zach added reluctantly.

Kane frantically scribbled on his pad whilst they all took turns around the table, recounting what they saw at Crooked House.

There were lots of tears, a few hugs and plenty of pizza shared amongst the group of friends. By the end of it, there were even a few jokes too. It was soothing, sharing their stories and feelings.

Nobody put on a brave front.

Nobody exaggerated.

They were all in this together, and everyone was heard.

Once everyone felt satisfied that they had captured everything, they turned to the files Izzy had taken with her. The pile sat neatly stacked in the middle of the table, all in numerical order thanks to her OCD.

33

"Let's start with room 6," Kane suggested.

Izzy opened the file and shared her findings.

None of them could figure out how someone had taken a picture of the missing girl a year before she went missing.

"The date stamp and the res definitely look like it's come from a security camera," JJ concluded. "What else is in the file?"

Izzy flicked through and pulled out three sheets of A4 paper, then carefully laid them out as if she was dealing up a game of solitaire.

"We have the newspaper clippings taken from the time of Jessica's disappearance, plus these handwritten notes." Izzy picked up the page, which looked like a diary extract, and read the contents aloud.

September 12th, 2011.

Another guest complained about strange scratching noises coming from the wardrobe in room 6 today. When I went to investigate, I could've sworn I heard a child sobbing, but we have no children staying with us at the moment, so I've started another one of my journals for the room and see where it takes me. I've called out pest control several times now, but they have failed to find anything other than extreme cold patches in certain parts of the house. Whilst this is all good for business and adds to our reputation of being haunted, I can't help but wonder what tragic secrets we've yet to unlock in this house.

October 31st, 2011.

It's Halloween and as usual the place is fully booked. Our guest in room 6 reported sobbing coming from his wardrobe. He didn't complain about it, instead he quizzed me about the history of the room. I gave him the generic answer I give all our guests, but when the room is vacant next, I intend to spend some time in there to see what I can find out. Helen and I bought this place to have a bit of fun. A spooky tourist attraction with the odd thing that went bump in the night, but things seem to have taken a far darker turn recently. The place has an edge to it now that's palpable and quite intimidating.

"This is the missing owner I read about in the article I found."

The sudden realization got the better of JJ's manners and he excitedly cut across Izzy's narration.

"Sorry Izzy, the point I was going to make was that he went missing in 2015, which means there might be a clue to what happened to him in these files."

"Keep reading Izzy," Kane interjected.

JJ's comment threatened to throw the room back into chaos, just when they had settled into some structure. Izzy's eyes quickly returned to the journal, to find where she had stopped.

THE RISING

November 3rd, 2011.

I finally got the chance to stay in room 6 last night, although I'm seriously regretting it now as I haven't slept a wink. Helen is out of town on one of her girly spa breaks, but when she gets back, we need to have a serious talk. I'm now certain something terrible is going on here in Crooked House.

I had just settled down into bed when I heard a slow, repetitive scratching noise coming from the wardrobe in the opposite corner of the room. Just as I placed my hand on the wardrobe door to look inside, the scratching stopped and I heard a child crying. I knew damn well the wardrobe was empty, as I'd checked when I first arrived. When I eventually plucked up the courage to open the door, the table lamp went out and I was plunged into complete darkness. I stupidly tripped over the corner of the bed, trying to make my way back to the main light and landed on all fours. After a couple of curses and a few shakes of my head, I felt an icy-cold hand grip my ankle, small like a child's hand. I leapt up and scrambled my way back to the light switch, only to find the room was empty, but the wardrobe door was wide open. I certainly hadn't opened it! Anyway, I made sure it was still empty, then closed it again and climbed back into bed. After an hour of silence, I eventually drifted off to sleep.

I awoke again at around 3am to a loud bang. The wardrobe door was open once more, and in the darkness of the hanging space I could just about make out a ruffle of yellow fabric poking out from the shadows. The wardrobe was definitely empty the last time I checked, so once again I jumped out of bed to investigate. As I got closer, something yanked the fabric back inside and the wardrobe door slammed shut behind it. I nearly had a heart attack.

It all happened so fast!

That's when I saw it. The open wardrobe door had hidden it before, but on the wall, someone had written the words 'help me' in crayon. I wonder if we should get in touch with that Peter chap again. I'm afraid something truly horrid is happening here, right under our noses.

November 10th, 2011.

Today Helen and I agreed to set up a hidden camera in room 6 and closed it to the public. There have been growing reports of disturbed sleep from our guests in this room and it's a fine line between being a quaint little haunted B&B and an uninhabitable one. Hopefully, we can see what's happening in that room.

November 13th, 2011.

I can't quite believe what I've seen today. When I checked the recording for room 6 this morning, I saw a tiny little girl in a yellow dress creep out of the wardrobe. She looked like an extra from a zombie movie; pale and covered in dirt. She toddled over to the window and then disappeared.

It looks like we may have had a power surge which interfered with the camera, as one minute she was there and the next she'd vanished. I checked for any signs of forced entry, but there was nothing.

I simply cannot understand how on earth she got in there unless she is some kind of ghost?

November 20th, 2011.

There have been no more sightings of the ghostly girl in room 6 so I have no choice but to open that room back up again. We just can't afford to lose any more revenue.

July 22nd, 2012.

I've not made any entries for a while now, despite there being lots of the usual creepy activity going on around the house. It's difficult enough running a B&B at the best of times, but a haunted one full of wannabe ghost hunters certainly keeps you on your toes and as a result, I've let this journal slip. A booming business is a nice problem to have, of course and I'm not complaining. That said, this week has shaken me to my core.

A young girl named Jessica went missing a couple of days ago and the police think she may have gotten herself lost in the woods. Her mum was busy checking in at the front office and when she turned around, she was gone.

I asked for a description and the mother showed me a picture of the same girl I watched wander out of the wardrobe in room 6 last year! I nearly threw up when I saw it was her.

We searched the house high and low, but she was nowhere to be found. The police inspector thinks she may have wandered outside to explore and got lost. Helen and I have helped with the search, along with other guests, but it's been two days now and still no trace of her anywhere. I daren't tell anyone about the video or the photo I have; they'll think I've taken her!

Or they'll think I'm mad.

Either way, they would lock me up!

We've closed room 6 again to see what the camera picks up.

I pray they find her soon.

August 18th, 2012.

It's been almost a month now and there is still no sign of little Jessica. The cameras haven't picked anything up *since that strange night in November and the world has moved on. Not my world, though. I'm convinced this place is connected to her disappearance somehow, so I've set up cameras in the rest of the rooms and will monitor them whenever they are vacant. Helen and I are increasingly distant, and she thinks I'm letting this place consume me. Maybe she's right. I just know there must be some kind of explanation for whatever's going on here.*

"That was the last entry for that room." Izzy shuffled the paperwork back into its original order and closed the file.

"This is crazy! Do you think the owner had anything to do with her going missing?" Meridia felt an unexplainable sense of attachment to Jessica since her last encounter, and the fact Jessica's mother was still out there after all these years, completely in the dark over what had happened, upset her deeply.

"We need to go through the other files," Kane was wide-eyed and brimming with newfound enthusiasm at the growing mystery.

"It's our only hope of getting any answers. Let's each take two and take turns reading them. We should do the rest in order to avoid confusion. I'll take room 1." Kane pulled the file over toward him and began by placing a photo down face up on the table.

The guest in room 1 was an average looking, middle-aged man. He had a trimmed beard and balding head, which reflected the sunlight creeping in from the window behind him.

Kane wasn't sure what he was expecting, but there was nothing remarkable or suspicious about the picture to begin with.

"Should we be looking for anything specific?" Zach asked.

"I guess we should just call stuff out that might be relevant?" Kane replied, shrugging his shoulders.

"Wait, look at his hands," Zach pointed at the bottom of the picture. "Is that blood?" he asked, noticing that the man's palms were facing the camera and stained a dark cherry red.

"It looks like it," Kane replied. "Great spot spud."

The photo had a very solemn feel to it, and even though the man's face was masked by a shadow from the light pouring in behind him, it was clear he was melancholy, as if he was in mourning.

His body looked weary, and his posture was that of pure dejection.

"He looks so sad...What else is in the file?" Meridia was keen to find out more.

Kane sifted through the file and retrieved the lone extra piece of paper.

"No press cuttings for this guy, I'm afraid. We don't even have a name. All we have is a few short diary notes like the ones for room 6." Kane read it to himself at first and then stopped when he felt the eyes of the group boring into him. "Sorry guys, my bad."

June 2nd, 2009.

A paranormal expert came to stay last night, and he suggested we keep a diary of any strange occurrences in the house, so here we are. He was pretty tight-lipped about what he experienced in this room, but whatever happened was enough to spook him. I saw him speaking to a few other guests over breakfast early this morning, and then he checked out. When I remade his bed, I noticed a chill in there, despite it being the start of summer. Perhaps I'm coming down with something, but I thought I'd better make a note of it, anyway.

June 16th, 2009.

I've decided not to report every incident in these files, as I would spend all my hours writing. Since the paranormal expert stayed, we seem to get more and more reports of strange, shadowy figures around the house at night. The latest guest in room 1 insisted on being moved in the early hours of this morning. Apparently, they awoke to find a bright-eyed monster staring at them from the foot of the bed. Its eyes were glowing in the dark! I expect it was a dream, but I moved her anyway. The customer is always right, as they say...

September 15th, 2013.

Of all the rooms, this has been the quietest, so has had little of my attention lately. Last night, however, when the room was vacant, the camera caught the image of a man. It was just fleeting, and I wasn't sure if I was seeing things at first, but upon pausing the recording, I could see him clear as day. I have no idea who he is or where he came from, but the last time we caught someone on camera, tragedy followed soon after.

I must remain vigilant, but I have nobody to turn to with this. Things are strained between Helen and I and so I don't want to burden her with any of it.

I'm worried I may be losing my mind.

"That's it for this one, guys. The last entry is two years before the owner disappeared. What have we got in room 2?" Meridia opened the file and pulled out the contents.

"Not much in this one, I'm afraid; just a photo and a couple of notes." She placed the image on the table so everyone could see. It featured a young woman sitting on the edge of the bed with her head in her hands. Wearing an old-fashioned dress and matching corset, she looked like she was getting ready for a costume party. It reminded Izzy of a painting she'd seen on a school trip to the national art gallery called *The Servant Girl*.

"She reminds me of Cinderella," Meridia quipped.

"Look at the window behind her," Zach once again had spotted something the others hadn't.

A vague outline of the mystery woman's reflection could be seen in the window behind her, but instead of mirroring her pose, it had its head turned and was looking right at her.

Meridia felt a cold shiver scuttle its way up from between her shoulder blades and tickle the back of her neck.

"She looks like a witch."

"Things are getting pretty real here guys. Should we be taking this stuff to the police?" JJ blurted.

"Nobody is ever going to believe us, mate. It happens in almost every horror movie I've ever seen. The kids go to the police, get told off for trying to prank them and then end up grounded. Then they all die! Does anyone here want to be grounded?" Kane's reply was quick and cutting, although half in jest.

"Let's get to the end of the files and then take a vote on what we do next; deal?"

The group all nodded in agreement. "What do the notes tell us?"

"Just two entries, by the looks of it."

June 2nd, 2009.

I thought it would be easier to keep a separate journal for each room, given they all have very different personalities. Of course, I may be making a rod for my own back here, but we'll see.

So, just to recap; disturbances in this room all tend to occur at 3am. We've had countless guests claim to have woken up drenched in sweat as if we'd left the heating on all night. Back when we bought this place, our surveyor told us there were signs of a fire in this part of the house, but we've found no information about when that might have occurred.

Beyond that, Helen and I have smelt burning in there from time to time; usually when we've been cleaning.

Overall, this room seems to do just enough to unsettle, but not quite enough to drive someone out completely. As a result, we have guests regularly requesting it when they stay. In fact, one older couple stays there every year on their anniversary, and they haven't complained once.

January 5th, 2014.

Our camera finally captured the ghost in room 2 last night! I was reviewing the footage after my rounds and clearly saw a woman crying at the edge of the bed. I've taken a still and added it to this file.

Once again, it was fleeting and interrupted by a sudden surge of power. I'm now convinced these apparitions are the source of that power, but I'm still none the wiser about who they are or where they come from.

All I know is that there has been a spike in activity recently and the last time that happened was around the time Jessica went missing!

"That's all we have." Meridia closed the file and placed it on top of the ones they had already examined.

"So far it seems the only one they had concrete information on was Jessica," Kane stood up and began pacing as his mind searched for some dots to connect. "We're getting closer to the owner's disappearance now, but no closer to understanding what happened today. JJ, what's in the third file?"

JJ swivelled the folder around on the table until it faced him and slowly opened it. They all shifted their attention to the next photo in line which looked like it had been taken during an earthquake.

Room 3 was a blur of frenetic motion. Its swirling cyclone of pinks and blues looked almost artistic, and in the centre of the storm stood a man in khaki military garb. He looked rigid, beyond the obvious nature of any photograph, and was screaming at the heavens in torment.

"There aren't any notes in this like the others," JJ proclaimed in disappointment. He turned the picture over and read out the handwritten note on the back, *"Private William Spencer, MIA 1944?* One article I read said Crooked House was used in the war. Maybe this is a ghost from back then?"

"I wonder why the question mark, though." Zach mumbled, "And how come there aren't any notes?"

"What does the date stamp say on the photo, mate?" Kane was hoping it would give them some insight.

"It's dated February 15th, 2016. So that's an entire year after the first owner disappeared."

"Maybe his wife carried on watching the rooms after he went missing?" Kane quickly scribbled the soldier's name in his notebook. "What's behind door number 4?" he joked in his best mock game show host voice.

An uncomfortable cloud of hush descended on the group as they all soaked up the photo in front of them.

Room 4 had the clearest image they had seen so far.

The guest was a powerful-looking man somewhere in his thirties. A long thin scar severed his left eyebrow, disappearing into the shadow of his deep-sunken eyes, which looked like empty sockets. He stood dead centre of the room, staring directly into the camera, devoid of any emotion. Atop of his chiselled, clean-shaven face, his hair was a shock of pure white which stood up on end like a match's flame. He was dressed entirely in black with short sleeves which emphasized the size of his sculpted biceps.

"How creepy is he?!" declared JJ. "He has the same weird eyes as the monsters. I wonder who he is?"

Kane thought he looked strangely familiar, but kept his thoughts to himself. His tired brain was feeling the effects of information overload, and he wanted to keep everyone focused on the task in hand.

"What do the notes say, Zach?" Zach pulled out the only other page in the file and scanned it,

"This goes back to the beginning again."

June 2nd, 2009.

Room 4 is by far the creepiest room in the house and is a fan favourite. Along with being nigh on impossible to warm, the room has played host to many ghost sightings. The most common reports from guests have all involved waking up to a shadowy figure looming over them menacingly. Several people have also claimed to see a group of children standing in the corner furthest from the door.

There are no records of anything specific happening in this room, but in the 70s there were a series of grisly child

murders in the area, and I often wonder if there is any connection.

I always feel a strong sense of dread whenever I enter this room, and Helen has boycotted it altogether, saying she always feels like someone is watching her whenever she's cleaning in there.

Of all the rooms in Crooked House, this is by far the most active all year round.

It's also the most unnerving.

August 20th, 2012.

I didn't have to wait very long for the camera to pick something up in this room, and I can't say I'm surprised. I have no clue who this ghost is, but one thing is for sure: he's intimidating.

Since my last entry, I did a bit of research into the killer in the 70s. Locals said he claimed at least 5 children in the area, although that number could never be verified as no bodies were ever found. Running circles around the police, he remained an enigma, sending disturbing photos to his victims' families. He was nicknamed 'The Demon of Cold Christmas' by the press and mysteriously disappeared after a year-long reign of terror.

My gut is telling me this is our guy, but there were never any witnesses when he was active.

If it is him, then I wonder why he is here.

May 23rd, 2014.

Another hit, this time a group of children loitering in the room's corner. I counted five in this photo, and they must be his victims. I knew something bad was on the horizon and this...

"Wait! Is there another picture in the file?" Izzy was the first to react, having listened intently to Zach's every word.

Zach located a second image that had fallen to the bottom of the file. He fished it out and placed it on the table for all to see.

A second wave of silence swept across the room as the group contemplated what was in front of them.

Congregating in the far corner of room 4, just as the owner had described, were a handful of children. Lank, bloodless faces stared into space like zombies searching for their next meal.

Meridia looked at the children in the photo and then slowly surveyed the group around her.

"They look like us...I mean...they look like they could be our age."

Zach began to squirm and fidget in his chair, trying to prevent Meridia's comment from crawling any further underneath his skin.

"I don't want to end up like them...lost in those woods somewhere...just a ghost locked in a wardrobe or left to wander the halls of an abandoned house!" Meridia was teetering on the edge of hysterics as shock took its hold.

Clenching her fists to stop her hands from shaking, she looked around the table for a show of support. She needed to hear everything was going to be ok. She needed to believe it. Zach was staring back at her, deeply moved by her anguish; his puppy dog eyes were wide and welling up.

"It's going to be ok Meridia...we're going to get through this. We never have to go back to that place ever again now. All we're doing right now is piecing together a mystery. Nothing more than that." Kane tried to settle her nerves as she rocked back and forth in her chair, her mind elsewhere as it raced ahead of everyone in the pursuit of tragic outcomes.

"Do you want me to take over, mate?" Sensing he'd been rattled, JJ offered to give Zach some respite from what was by far the most disturbing file they had opened.

"It's ok…I don't mind. Shall I carry on reading?"

The group gave their approval with silent nods, still hypnotized by the malignant images in front of them.

"…must be his victims…I…I knew something bad was on the horizon and this proves it. There is something evil in this house. I can feel it, and I think it lives in room 4."

December 31st, 2014.

It's New Year's Eve, and the house is quiet. Things have been rough the last few months and I wonder if I'm losing my grip on reality. I keep seeing shadows all around the house, in the halls, in my room at night. My nerves are completely shredded now and I'm constantly looking over my shoulder waiting for something bad to happen.

I've decided this will be my last journal entry as tomorrow the house will be completely empty and I'm going to put an end to this once and for all.

Helen will drive to her mother's in the morning, and I will meet her later that day. By then, this place will be nothing but ash.

Crooked House is pure evil.

I can feel it tightening its grip on me and the people of Cold Christmas. It must be stopped before it's too late. There's a monster in here. The most terrifying monster I've ever seen.

Nobody is safe anymore.

Not me, not Helen, and not our guests.

Room 4 is at the heart of it. He stands there every

night, watching me, taunting me. That killer, and God knows what demon he has summoned.

It all ends tonight!

"There are no more entries after that." Zach closed the file and stared at his feet under the table whilst trying to compose himself. His long, unkempt fringe covered the tears that had returned to the corners of his eyes.

"See! What are we doing here, guys? This is serious! People have died and gone missing. There must be someone we can go to for help..." Meridia rose to her feet, anxious and unsettled again. "We're just kids...a bunch of dumb kids...what can we do?"

"We're all upset...I get it. But look what we've already done. We got out. That's already more than a lot of adults have been able to do. We must assume the house took the owner the same way it tried to take us. In fact, I bet he went missing the very next day after writing that note." Kane was trying to pull everyone's attention back to the mystery that was unfolding in front of them, and away from the danger they had all exposed themselves to.

He reached for the file on room 5 and pulled it closer to him.

"We need to finish looking at these files, then we can decide who we go to. We only know half the story at the moment. Maybe the answers we're looking for are in the rest of these files."

He opened the file and pulled out the next image. It was as haunting as it was disturbing.

A young woman was wide-eyed and screaming for her life as she rushed towards the camera. Ebony eyes, full of terror, glistened in the dimly lit room, while her furrowed brow begged for mercy. Frozen in perpetual torment, long brunet hair which ebbed away wildly in all directions framed her distraught expression as if she was secretly clutching a plasma ball.

"It looks like she's being chased by something," JJ speculated. They all studied the tiny goldfish bowl room behind her in search of a clue, but it was empty.

"She looks petrified," Izzy stated the obvious.

"It's more than that though, Izz," Merdia reengaged tentatively, "there's a sadness to her; it's like she can't take any more and just wants to be put out of her misery."

"Another one with no notes I'm afraid so we'll never know," exclaimed Kane as he shook the file over the table to demonstrate. "The date stamp is from 2016 again, so after the owner's disappearance."

"Izz, are there any more notes in the files we have left?" Meridia felt her impatience bubbling. She had always been a 'go big or go home' kind of girl, and if she was going to keep going, then she needed to know what else was looming on the horizon.

"I never looked. I was only interested in room 6 when we were back at the house." Izzy felt around in each of the remaining files to find there were no more notes in any of them. All they had to go on now were cryptic photographs.

"Well, that's burst my bubble," Kane quipped in an attempt to win back his audience. "Let's look at the last of the photos and figure out what we do next, shall we?"

Izzy pushed the image from room 7 to the centre of the table so everyone got a clear view.

"Shit! I know who that guy is. I've seen him before." JJ exclaimed from his corner of the table as he fumbled for his phone. "He's the owner. That's Jonathan Ashfield. Look!" he thrust his phone out so everyone could see his screen, and there in the original article, the one that had led them to this madness, was the same man they were now staring at on a CCTV still.

"Oh god...that's awful. Izz, put it away...please..." the shocking image visibly shook Meridia.

Jonathan Ashfield was now the ghost in room 7 and provided them with the most horrific picture they had seen so far.

The man's neck was snapped to one side, leaving his head perched on his left shoulder. His face was freakishly twisted in fear as if something had literally scared him to death mid-scream. White eyes, rolled back in their sockets, pointed towards the window as he sat slumped lifeless in the room's corner.

Izzy turned the photograph over, which revealed a note written on the back which said

Jonathan Ashfield; missing and presumed dead January 1st, 2015.

The room collapsed into stony silence as they mourned their late reporter.

"Kane's right, we need to look at the others so we can decide what to do." JJ's uncharacteristically solemn tone cut through the silence and stirred everyone from the grave bewilderment they had slipped into. "I know it's tough, but we're here now. We're safe. We've got to keep going."

Zach tentatively reached for the file on room 8, which sat in front of Izzy.

She fired an apprehensive glance in Meridia's direction and then watched as Zach dragged the file over to where he was sitting.

He pulled out the latest picture and reluctantly turned it over for all to see.

While the photo of room 8 was still disturbing, it offered the group brief respite after the harrowing image of Jonathan Ashfield moments earlier. It featured an old woman propped up in bed. Her face was overcast with shadows, and it looked like the image had been captured at night. Surrounded by heavy bags of loose sallow flesh, her bulging eyes were wide and luminous, whilst her expression remained deadpan and soulless. Bedraggled white hair finished her nightmarish look, giving the impression she had just sat bolt upright amid a bad dream.

"I feel like she's staring right at me," JJ gasped, and the group all agreed. It was a haunting picture, which made the hairs on the back of Meridia's neck stand to attention once again. She had a bad feeling about this woman and couldn't quite fathom why.

"What's wrong, Meridia?" Zach quizzed with a tinge of concern.

"I don't know. There's something about her that gives me the creeps, and it's more than how she looks. This is going to sound mad, but this one scares me more than the last."

"Look! Did anyone see that?" JJ stood up in a panic, knocking his chair over behind him as he did.

"What? Mate, see what?" Kane was the first to respond as JJ's unexpected agitation became contagious and swept its way around the table.

"There!" JJ pointed at the photo in front of Zach, causing him to flinch away from it too. "Her eyes...they moved. I swear...she looked right at me as soon as I spoke."

JJ's claim put everyone on high alert, particularly

Meridia, as she latched onto Izzy's hand in fear while they all gazed at the old woman in front of them.

"It's been a long day mate, and we're all jumpy..." Kane tried to diffuse the tension.

"I swear mate! She looked right at me...as if she heard what I said." JJ wasn't budging.

"Let's put that one away for now. It might have been..."

"What? A trick of the light? Maybe...but I swear her eyes moved."

"Do we need a minute? I don't mind guys...maybe grab a refill from the fridge and stretch our legs?" As Kane continued to play things down, Zach turned the photo face down.

"We've come this far...let's just get it over with. Just keep that picture away from me!" Seeing JJ was visibly flustered, Zach decided to put the picture back in its file.

"One more to go." Kane pressed on, sighing as he revealed the last image.

A chorus of gasps erupted as they all came face to face with the bloodbath in room 9. Blood spattered and smeared the dreary, off-white walls, while a gory crimson sea covered the stony floor. Hand painted on the mirror above the bed, an ominous message said...

TOO LATE!

"Oh my god, there's so much blood...even the writing..." Zach blurted, reeling from shock.

"This is real guys...that's somebody's blood on the floor." The grisly nature of the image rattled Izzy.

"It looks like a murder scene from a movie...but I can't see anyone in there." Kane concluded.

At first glance, the room did indeed look empty, which

was out of keeping with all the other photos they'd seen. The group all crowded in to get a closer look, as if playing a morbid version of '*Where's Wally*'.

"There, under the bed," exclaimed Zach.

He was always good at playing that game, much to the annoyance of Kane.

Hiding in the shadows, under the blood-soaked bed, was a young boy. All they could see was his face from the eyes down, but at a guess, he looked a similar age to them. Despite the carnage around him, he didn't look afraid though, more mischievous in Meridia's eyes.

"This one is dated December 2022," Kane read from the back of the print. "That's pretty recent compared to some others, and after the owner's wife, Helen, went missing."

"Do you think he was murdered there?" Zach asked.

"There's just no way of knowing who he is, or what he's doing there." Kane replied.

His flippant response encapsulated their findings, as despite the various journal entries and Jessica's press clippings, it still felt as if they were looking at nine jigsaw pieces without possessing the box they came in.

"So, whose cameras, are they?" Zach asked.

"The same person who is keeping these files, I guess."

"But why?"

"Maybe the owner's wife isn't really missing?" Meridia proposed.

"Or maybe whoever is watching the place did something to her?"

Kane was quiet. He was busy processing everything they'd uncovered and trying to match it against his extensive knowledge of the horror genre. His train of thought was interrupted by Izzy, who'd had an epiphany.

"We have nine pictures and ten folders. Based on the puppet show you both saw and the owner's journals, I think we can assume the monsters we saw took that girl in room 6. So, what if the monsters have been gradually filling up the rooms with people? That would explain why they said they had been waiting for Zach."

An awkward silence befell the room as everyone looked at Zach.

Izzy was not known for her diplomacy, but she meant no one any harm. She just had a habit of skipping a filter or two whenever she got excited.

"We need to get rid of the elephant in the room guys," Kane broke the silence. "We all saw some kind of creepy version of Zach in there, and we're all worried about what he said. Sorry, bro."

He gave his brother a playful wink and hoped trivializing things might settle his nerves.

"We've gone through all the files now and know that place is evil. It's taken at least nine people so far and locked them away in its rooms for whatever reason. Maybe it is the monsters we saw, maybe it's the psycho in room 4 and he's running the show.

What we know is Jessica went missing at least 10 years ago and yet we've caught her on video today, so that's evidence nobody can refute. Anyone can Photoshop some pictures in a file, but what we have is much harder to fake. Plus, we've seen her up close, and she still looks 6 years old. She also had the same creepy eyes as the monsters and 'spooky Zach' did. We don't know what that means, or how that's even possible at the moment.

None of this seems possible! Time travel?

The owner saw Jessica way before she went missing, so it's not that far-fetched.

Maybe Crooked House was built on some kind of wormhole or something? We just don't know.

I think Izzy's right though. We have to assume whatever is behind all this is now gunning for Zach, but we stopped it. Whoever has been keeping these files has more answers than we do so we need to find out who that...."

Kane trailed off mid-sentence and the colour drained from his face as if he was about to pass out

"What if they were watching us there today? We could all be in danger right now!"

34

"But how would they know who we are?" Meridia asked.

"We posted the video on our channel when you went missing."

"What?!"

"Wait, it's not like that. We posted it as an insurance policy...in case anything happened to us, too. We thought at least that way someone might have seen it and come looking for us...we all agreed it was a good idea at the time."

"I guess that makes sense," Meridia conceded, as her cheeks cooled and returned to their usual colour. "Has anyone seen it?"

"Let's take a look," Kane said, disappearing to fetch his laptop.

He re-emerged a few minutes later, cradling his open laptop and looking pale again.

"We have a real problem now guys," he stuttered as he placed the laptop on the table for all to see.

"120 views! Wow!" JJ gushed.

"No! Look at the comments..." Kane pointed to the screen. His hands were shaking.

All the comments were from people purporting to have seen a shadow monster in their house since watching the video. Meridia's return to the house coincided with the appearance of shadow creatures in every viewer's video.

'I just watched your video and noticed a dark figure in my doorway.'

'Just seen a shadow person in my bedroom! #scarytales'

'DO NOT WATCH THIS VIDEO! THIS CHANNEL IS EVIL!'

"It's got to be a prank," Izzy piped up.

"That's what I thought until I saw this." Kane scrolled down and hit a video link someone had posted in the comments section.

The clip opened with a teenage girl under her duvet talking directly into the camera.

"So, I've just watched the latest Scarytales video that's trending and we're about to see if it's all a big hoax."

The group watched on in anticipation as she rotated her camera view and slowly pulled the covers down. Her heavy duvet scraped the phone's mic, overloading the audio, as the pulsating lens struggled to adapt to her dimly lit bedroom.

"Nothing so far..." She giggled as she conducted a mock-search of her room.

Izzy could feel the onset of motion sickness as the blur of lights and shadows shakily raced left, then right.

Suddenly, the camera came to a jarring halt. There, in

the corner of her room, wedged between her desk and the wall, was one of the creatures.

A soundtrack of screams and panic played out as the camera shook, as if they were witnessing things from the inside of a washing machine on its spin cycle.

Once the commotion had settled, the camera regained its focus. All they could hear now was the girl frantically trying to catch her breath. The creature lingered, staring at her with god-awful eyes, then vanished through the wall like a ghost.

Kane pressed stop.

"What have we done?!" Meridia gasped in horror. "You need to take it down now!"

Kane scrolled down to the end of the comments when he noticed a new one had appeared.

'You need to take this video down now! You're all in grave danger. I'll meet you outside Crooked House tomorrow morning at 10am to explain everything. Sincerely, Peter Higginsworth'

35

Peter Higginsworth finished typing his message and hit 'post'.

He printed a screen shot of Zach's doppelgänger from earlier that day. He'd been praying for this moment to come; the slimmest of chances to bring the evil onslaught of Crooked House to a grinding halt. Years of watching from the safety of his own shadows had brought him here.

He felt flush, and a little dizzy as the significance of today's events caught up with him.

A juddering drone broke the silence as his printer robotically spat out the image of the latest occupant; a local boy who looked no more than 11 years old.

Peter wondered if he had the strength to do what was needed.

"So, you are the final piece of this terrible puzzle," he said to himself, still staring at Zach's haunting face.

"You're going to be too late again," whispered the voice behind him. Peter swivelled around in his chair to meet his unwanted visitor.

"I won't," he replied.

Standing in the doorway was the same shadowy creature Kane had seen in his video comments. Its raven eyes sparkled in the gloom as it stared intently at Peter.

Peter rose from his chair and picked up the printed image for his file on room 10. He walked right at the unwelcome spectre in a mental game of chicken.

"We'll see this time," he said, and with false bravado, strolled right through the visitor.

On impact the shadow monster evaporate like smoke, and Peter was alone once more.

36

Mr and Mrs Jackson returned home from their shopping trip at around 9pm that evening, and it provided the perfect cue for everyone else to call it a day. Once they had said their goodbyes, Kane and Zach headed straight up to bed.

"I will not let anything happen to you, you know that, right?" Kane's words were a welcome boost before facing his room alone but also made Zach realize just how vulnerable he felt. "We got through today, didn't we? Besides, Peter will know what to do."

Kane placed a reassuring hand on his brother's shoulder and gave it an affectionate squeeze.

"We've got this…I promise. Now try to get some sleep; we've got a big day tomorrow."

"Thanks. I'll see you in the morning." Zach trundled off to his bedroom and closed the door.

All he thought about was the chilling message his gruesome double had delivered back at Crooked House. Inside, he went to his wardrobe and quickly found what he was looking for. He pulled out a brown wooden hanger holding a marled blue hoody and inspected it. He'd recognized it from back in room 6, and here it was right before his eyes, unworn with the price tags still attached.

"Sorry dad." He mumbled to himself as he wandered across the room and stuffed the sweater as far underneath his bed as his arm could stretch. He figured if he never wore it, then the bleak prediction they had all heard couldn't possibly come true. Satisfied with his logic, Zach turned the light out and climbed into bed.

He never had a problem with the dark before, but tonight his eyes scoured the room, straining to make out something soothing he could latch onto.

Shadows bled in and out of each other, painting an array of patterns in the room as his eyes struggled to adjust. A thin trail of pale-yellow light crept under his door from the landing outside, and he used that as a guide to find his bearings.

Within seconds he made out the white wooden desk opposite his bed, and from there the familiar shapes of his room all took shape. His laptop and monitor that sat atop his desk, the display shelf to the left, featuring his favourite superheroes, and his chest of drawers where he kept his video games in the farthest corner to his right. It all came together like a patchwork quilt of creature comforts.

That was until he spotted something within that quilt that didn't belong.

There, in the darkened corner next to his video games, a shape which was far darker than everything else appeared. A short, sharp pulsation of pure dread jolted his entire body as he strained to see what it was. Two tiny orbs of light appeared in response, unblinking, and Zach was no longer the only person staring.

He switched his bedside lamp on and whatever he thought was there vanished.

"Must be my eyes…playing tricks," he muttered. He relaxed his shoulders, which were now hunched around his ears, and did his best to let go of any tension he was carrying before turning the lamp off again.

Once more, he saw the glistening orbs staring back at him in the dark.

Shaking in fear, he reached out for his lamp and knocked it to the floor. Its light bounced off the dusty blue carpet and for a split-second Zach saw the creature from Crooked House looming over him beside his bed. Its arms raised high toward the ceiling, extending its razor-sharp fingers as if it was about the strike a killer blow.

"Aaaaah!" Zach clenched his eyes tight and screamed, a haunting, high-pitched scream that carried itself into Kane's room.

37

Kane heard the scream from next door and bolted out of bed.

Zach had a penchant for being dramatic, but given the horrors they'd both witnessed that day, he figured he deserved the benefit of the doubt.

As Kane entered, the hazy yellow glow of the landing nightlight leaked into Zach's bedroom, skimming his brother's quivering frame as he lay curled up facing the wall.

"You ok mate?" He whispered into the gloom, but Zach didn't answer.

As Kane edged closer, he felt a knot of guilt tighten deep in the pit of his stomach. It was his fault they'd all gone to that wretched place; all in the selfish pursuit of fame.

Resting a hand on his brother's shoulder, he whispered again, "Zach?"

But his brother wasn't in his bed.

He was standing in the doorway behind him, still brushing his teeth.

"What was that noise?" Zach asked innocently.

An ice-cold chill rippled up Kane's spine, one vertebra at a time, rooting him to the spot as the imposter rolled over to reveal himself. Crazed eyes full of rage glistened in the darkness, as the evil boyish creature bared its teeth and giggled; a demented, rasping giggle. With one vicious swipe of its razor-sharp claws, the creature lashed out, slicing Kane's throat to the bone.

KANE JUMPED UP IN BED, clasping his neck in panic.

"It was just a nightmare..." he gasped, but before he had time to dwell, another scream rang out from Zach's bedroom.

Kane leapt out of bed, battling against déjà vu to go to his brother's aid.

"What's wrong?!" he pleaded as his eyes darted around the room in search of danger. He felt his heart racing, but the monster from his dreams was nowhere to be found.

"It was in here! I saw it in the dark!" tears were streaming down Zach's distraught face as he teetered on the brink of hysteria.

"What was here? I can't see anything..."

"The monster! I saw it...It was right here," Kane continued to scan the room, but nothing looked out of place.

"Well, it's gone now, whatever it was. You're tired. How about I stay here until you fall asleep?"

Their dad's voice bellowed up the stairs, "Are you two ok up there?"

Kane twisted his neck and shouted back towards the open door. "It's ok dad, we were just messing around...going to bed now."

"I'm sure it was here.." Zach whimpered, beginning to doubt his own eyes.

"It's been a long day for all of us and we've all seen some scary shit. I bet none of us will get much sleep tonight, regardless of how brave we all think we are. Why don't you leave your lamp on and I'll stay here until you drift off?"

"Ok, thanks." Zach shuffled his body back down the bed and hid under his covers, whilst Kane sat on the floor next to him like a guard dog on the lookout for the first sign of trouble.

As he studied his brother's room, he realized how young they all were. Zach's shrine to video gaming, his superhero figurines all striking action-poses on the shelf above his desk, the secret stash of comics he knew he kept under his bed. All beloved trinkets from an era none of them were quite ready to relinquish.

How he longed to go back in time just one day and steer them all clear of that miserable place. His thirst for fame and followers had cost all five of them the twilight of their childhood, maybe even their lives.

How on earth would they ever stop the evil within Crooked House?

Five teens and an author!

What hope did they have?

"Summmmm...hithaff....gooooom," Kane's guilt was interrupted by Zach jabbering in his sleep.

"See! Just kids," he replied, half to himself.

Kane got up off the floor to find his brother sound asleep. "Sleep well, little man." He gently pulled the covers up a little higher under his chin and then hovered his hand over the bedside lamp. "I think we'll leave this on tonight, spud."

As he turned to make his way back to his own room, he

couldn't help but notice the marled blue hoodie hanging up on the outside of Zach's wardrobe.

The very sight of it sent an icy shiver down his spine. "You won't be wearing this anytime soon," he said, as he grabbed the wooden hanger on his way out.

38

JJ let out a tiny sigh of disappointment as he arrived home to a dark and empty house. Although it was pretty common for him during the week, tonight he'd hoped to see at least one of his parents before going to bed.

His mother worked long hours as a nurse at Chase Side Hospital and so often had little control over the hours she kept there. She was so passionate about her job and never said no to extra shifts, although she compensated by using the extra money she'd earn to buy JJ new gadgets here and there.

His love of tech had stemmed from that first tablet she bought him when he was at prep school. She'd been pulled into an all-nighter, and it was her way of saying sorry the next morning. He filled up the tablet's memory in a couple of days with random photos and videos he'd taken around the house.

The dynamic with his mum soon escalated into a self-fulfilling prophecy. She would buy him a gadget to justify her commitment to work, and he would spend the evenings using it to distract him from the emptiness he felt at home. It was a cliché, but their relationship now felt akin to two ships passing in the night, three if you counted his dad.

JJ's father didn't have quite the same noble cause to justify his absence from their family home. He worked as a sales rep for a corporate furniture company and so often stayed out late schmoozing clients to close contracts. JJ sensed he did it out of loneliness initially, but over time it had just become a habit, or perhaps an addiction.

It was saddening that three people who loved each other so much spent so little time together under the same roof. Hence, JJ had always enjoyed spending so much time with Kane. His house always felt more homely whenever he was there, and Kane's parents treated him as one of their own.

JJ poured himself a glass of water and trotted upstairs to his room.

It had been one heck of a day and he couldn't wait to climb into bed and reflect on everything that had happened. As much as his brain was still buzzing with a million questions and worries, he was much more a lark than an owl and appreciated the benefits of a good night's sleep. Knowing his usual eight hours might be a tall order, he slipped under the covers and folded his arms behind his head. The cool touch of his clean bedding was a welcome tonic to his aching limbs, and he immediately felt more at ease.

Gazing up at the ceiling, he tuned into his breathing and found a steady, relaxed rhythm, before allowing his thoughts to flow freely.

In one fell swoop, Crooked House had turned his entire world upside down and nearly got him and his friends killed. He couldn't fathom how the monster sucked all the fight right out of him without even trying.

JJ would have happily drifted into a deathly slumber in that gloomy hallway, underneath that willowy mass of shadow and bone. In fact, he'd never felt peace quite like it and was a far cry from the tumultuous cyclone of questions whirling around in his mind now.

Closing his eyes, he envisioned the monster looming over him, suffocating him with that hypnotic stare. The files, the disturbing images they had all seen tonight, was easy by comparison. If it wasn't for Meridia charging at it the way she did, who knows what might have happened. *'What ifs'* he thought to himself.

He still couldn't be sure who told him to strike the windows, either.

JJ initially thought it was his inner voice, but now he suspected it may have been someone else or something more sinister after seeing the files. It felt like they were all trapped in a horror movie. Those creatures and the way they reacted to sunlight; it was like they had stumbled into a vampire's nest that had been plaguing the village undetected.

His thoughts drifted to Zach.

Poor Zach.

Surely, he'd glimpsed his own impending death today. Nobody wanted to admit it, but they'd all seen and heard what happened to Jonathan Ashfield eight years earlier, not to mention Jessica.

JJ sensed his natural positivity being choked to death by guilt. It was the heaviest weight he carried. If only he'd kept his mouth shut and not mentioned that damn article, then they'd have never gone to that accursed place. Their hope for survival now depended on a stranger.

He hoped to God Peter could help them all.

A wave of exhaustion swept over JJ's body, triggering a heavy, lethargic blink. Closing his eyes, he eventually succumbed to the wave, riding it all the way into the open arms of sleep.

39

Jennifer and Robert Di Salvo's were doing what they did every Saturday night when Izzy arrived home: they were listening to music in the snug whilst enjoying a bottle of merlot. Izzy did her best to close the door as softly as possible and slip in undetected. Her only desire was to retreat to her room and hibernate until morning.

"Is that you, darling?" her mother's voice floated down the hall and apprehended Izzy at the bottom of the stairs.

"Yes mum, it's me," she replied reluctantly.

Izzy had an amazing home-life, one that most of her friends would kill for, and she loved her parents dearly, but tonight all she wanted to do was go to bed. She was always awful at hiding things from her parents, and often wondered if her mum had some kind of sixth sense.

"Come dear, we haven't seen you all day."

Izzy trudged towards the snug, trying to think of something mundane to tell her parents about her day. She hated lying to them, but tonight had to be an exception. As she peered around the corner, her parents were in their usual position; curled up together on the plush grey sofa closest to the speaker. They regularly escaped work pressures in the snug, winding down on Saturday nights listening to jazz and indulging in an extra-large glass of wine.

"Hey guys," Izzy perked herself up as best she could, given the circumstances. Leanne Carroll was playing in the background and any other time, Izzy would have curled up on the opposing sofa and joined them for a while.

"I'm so tired, mum. We've been working on our school project all day and I feel ready for bed. How has your day been?" Izzy thought she'd try a different approach today and throw the attention on them to avoid suspicion.

"We've been fine, dear, just our usual Saturday. Your father played a round of golf while I caught up with Lidia, and we've spent the rest of the evening relaxing in here. Are you sure you don't want to join us for a while before bed?"

"I'm ok thanks. My eyes are tired so I'm just going to get an early night. I've said I'd go back to Zach's tomorrow to get it finished…I hope that's ok?"

"Of course, honey," Robert answered, "I can give you a lift there if you'd like?"

"It's ok dad, I said I'd knock for Meridia on the way, and we'd walk round together. Thanks though."

"That means your taxi service is no longer needed in the morning, handsome. How about a little top up?" Izzy's mum reached over for the bottle, and as she did, Izzy swept in and gave her an enormous hug and a kiss.

"What's that for, darling?" she said in surprise.

"Just missed you both today, that's all." She gave her dad a big squeeze and said goodnight, then wearily made her way to her bedroom.

By the time Izzy was ready for bed, she found she was surprisingly tired, despite the fact so much was still up in the air. Leaving things unresolved bothered her, and despite going through all the files and photos earlier, they still had more questions than answers.

Strangely, she had accepted the paranormal aspects of the day's revelations. The monsters, the ghosts, they were all irrefutable now.

She'd seen them.

She'd felt them.

It was the motives that bothered her, and that's where they had all drawn a blank.

If she was right and the sinister forces behind this waking nightmare were looking to fill Crooked House with the souls of innocents, then why? And why Zach? How on earth had Zach been in two places at once, and where did he and Kane go when they disappeared in the office for all that time?

Izzy breathed in a long, deep breath in frustration and pushed it out noisily through her nose. She lay there alone, tying her brain in knots like a pretzel for hours; hypothesizing and speculating over every possible outcome until she wore herself out completely. The last thing she saw was her bedside clock blinking 1:24am before fatigue took over and she finally drifted off to sleep.

40

When Meridia arrived home, the first thing she did was run to the kitchen and give her mum a big cuddle.

"What's this for M?" As tactile as Meridia was, her mum was still pleasantly surprised by her daughter's sudden urge.

"Missed you today, mum...that's all."

"Maybe you should spend the day round Zach's more often?" Emily Wilson winked, then gave Meridia a big cuddle of her own.

Emily looked more like Meridia's older sister than her mum. She'd had her at twenty, after marrying her childhood sweetheart, and time had been kind to her. They shared the same fiery red hair and piercing blue eyes, and both wore their heart on their sleeve.

She inherited little from her father in looks, except for his height, or rather, lack of it. She most certainly had his temper though, and that scared her. She constantly worried that she might end up like him, angry at the world and consumed with envy. Although she did her best to stay level-headed, she'd felt her temper boil over on many occasions that day, although she reasoned that was justified given everything that had happened.

"Do you want a hot chocolate before bed?" Emily assumptively flicked the switch at the bottom of the kettle in anticipation of her answer.

"No thanks. I think I'm just going to head up to bed if that's ok? My brain is fried from schoolwork today." Meridia felt guilty the moment the words left her mouth.

Since the incident with her dad, she'd always stayed up as late as she could to keep her mum company. She hated the thought of leaving her downstairs on her own to dwell on things. All she wanted to do was say yes to the hot chocolate and tell her mum everything that had happened, but that just wasn't possible. Not right now, anyway.

"Of course, hon. You go up and I'll bring a hot chocolate up for you to keep by your bed in case you change your mind. I'm just going to watch a little tv and then maybe get an early night myself. Us Wilson women need our beauty sleep after all." She gave Meridia another squeeze and fetched a bucket-sized mug down from the cupboard.

"Thanks, mum." Meridia dragged herself out of the kitchen and clambered up the stairs to get ready for bed.

The Wilson house was a modest sized two-up two-down, and Meridia's bedroom was the smallest of the two, but she preferred it that way. There was something about the closed in nature of it that made her feel safe. It was her haven.

As promised, her mum delivered one steaming hot cup of chocolate, full to the brim with marshmallows, followed by a tender kiss goodnight.

"I'll be up soon, sweetie. Sleep well."

It was a standing joke in her family that Wilson women fell asleep anywhere, even standing up, and Meridia was no exception. Once she was safely wrapped up in her marshmallow duvet and surrounded by the familiar amber glow of her Luna nightlight she drifted soundly off to sleep.

"*Meridia.....help me....*" Jessica's ethereal voice snaked and swirled around the room like a lost soul in search of a new host. "*Help me...please...*"

The ghostly SOS infiltrated Meridia's slumber and began worming its way toward her dreams. Having sought refuge in a treasured childhood memory, Meridia's saccharine fortress of nostalgia swiftly melted away, leaving her marooned in a cold and desolate hotel room that looked all too familiar.

Once again Jessica emerged from the shadows to greet her, and as the moonlight glanced her sallow face, the day's nightmarish events that sleep had magically staved off, all came flooding back.

"What do you want?" Meridia felt her voice pulsate and echo inside her head as if she'd spoken underwater. "I'm dreaming," she thought dubiously.

"*You need to see...*" The ghoul's blue, lifeless lips were unmoving, but Meridia heard her all the same.

"It must be a dream," she reasoned with a little more confidence.

Jessica gestured towards the door, which was now ajar and letting a faint amber light permeate the room.

"*Run! It's coming.*"

As Meridia clambered off the lumpy mattress, she noticed her cozy tartan pyjamas had been replaced by a pretty yellow summer dress. Confused, she looked back at her host Jessica for an explanation, but the spectre had vanished, leaving Meridia to face the rest of Crooked House alone.

"It's just a dream...it's just a dream..." she began

repeating the words like a mantra, as any composure she had gathered now threatened to abandon her. She heard the sharp scraping of nails on wood from the corner of the room.

"The wardrobe!"

The large oak frame began to rock and creak, as if something inside was trying to force its way out. It banged, and it clattered against the cold, hard floor, almost toppling over, as the violence trapped inside grew more and more determined to escape.

Each thunderous *crash* shook Meridia's entire body as she backed away towards her only exit. Blindly waving her arm behind her in search of the door, she felt the cold brass handle press against her palm and the wardrobe stopped shaking. Caught between a rock and a hard place, she waited in silence for what felt like a lifetime.

"Wake up Meridia! Wake up...this is just a dream," she told herself as she stayed deadlocked, not wanting to find out what other dangers might be lurking in the halls of Crooked House.

The towering wardrobe pivoted to face her, its right leg scraping across the stony ground before coming to a sharp halt.

Meridia's heart felt as if it was on the brink of bursting out of her chest, but still she clung onto the door handle behind her, unable to move from fear. A slow *creak* cut through the silence as the oak door in front of her opened. Jagged fingernails from within menacingly wrapped around the heavy wood, each landing with an ominous *click*.

That was all the incentive Meridia needed to flee. In search of an exit, she swiftly made her way into the hallway and sprinted along the corridor.

"Jesssicaaaaa....Jessssicaaaaaaaaaa....I caaaan smell your blood...."

The disjointed and disconnected voice sent a shockwave of panic rippling through Meridia's mind. Having run straight into a dead end, her only option now was to hide. She wracked her brain to remember the occupants in each room, but everything felt muddled and sluggish. Time was running out as the calling grew louder behind her.

"Jesssicaaaaa....come heeeere Jesssicaaaaa..."

"Room 8 it is," she thought as she pressed an ear to the door. A faint mechanical sound came from the other side, and it reminded Meridia of a late-night hospital drama she used to watch with her mum.

Turning the handle, she opened the door and slipped inside. Meridia didn't hear the boy's voice until it was too late, and she had already closed the door behind her.

"No! Not that room! You mustn't let her see you!"

Meridia scanned the room for any imminent danger and found that room 8 was sparse compared to the one she had just escaped. A large antique fourposter bed dominated proceedings, and there wasn't much space for anything else. The strange mechanical noise Meridia had heard from outside had stopped the moment she'd entered, and the dim moonlight creeping in through the room's only window cast a soft shadow across the bed covers, revealing someone laying under them.

"The old woman!" she remembered, and as she did, the elderly woman sat bolt upright and opened her eyes. Her icy white stare found Meridia in the shadows and stopped her in her tracks like a gorgon's gaze.

"Help me..." she croaked. *"Please help me..."* The old woman's voice was frail and full of self-pity.

Meridia felt compelled to move closer, as if a supernatural force was pulling her toward the bed. She opened her mouth to speak, but before she uttered a word, she felt a cold and clammy hand clasp her wrist and yank her out of the room.

"You must wake up," came the boy's voice again, but he was nowhere to be seen.

Instead, she found herself alone in total darkness.

"Where am I?" she asked.

"You must go. You must wake up before they find you," the boy implored, and as he spoke, an amber light flickered a few hundred yards ahead of her.

The dim light revealed an unfamiliar passageway that wouldn't have looked out of place in a castle. Old, mould-covered cobblestones paved a narrow brick hallway with a series of tiny openings on either side, like those found in a medieval dungeon.

"You must go now. They are coming."

Meridia felt a gentle nudge in the small of her back urging her forward.

She set off toward the light tentatively at first, edging her way down the corridor until she reached the first pair of openings. They were a little too high for her to see inside, but each had a brass number nailed above it.

Meridia counted ahead, and there were ten openings, one for each of the rooms in Crooked House.

She paused for a moment between numbers 1 and 2, battling hard against her foggy memory to recall who occupied those particular rooms, but try as she might, Meridia just couldn't focus.

Creeping closer to the opening marked 1, she realized if she stood on her tiptoes, she might be able to peek inside. The corridor was deathly silent and as much as she knew she had to keep moving, common sense succumbed to curiosity and she ventured closer to the dark cavity.

"It's just a dream," she thought, as she got within touching distance of the opening.

Meridia hesitated and looked around, certain she'd heard the faintest of noises coming from behind her, but the corridor was still empty. Plucking up the courage to investigate, she extended her arms out above her shoulders.

"If I can just grab that ledge, I'll be able to hoist myself up to see," but as she got close enough a man's arm burst out of the darkness, his large blood-stained hand swung wildly, snatching at the air. Meridia felt the gentle breeze it caused brush against her face and fell backwards with a bump, jarring her coccyx on the unforgiving ground.

Despite her insistence she was dreaming, the pain felt very real and went soaring up her spine, making her wince.

The rest of the corridor erupted in a deafening cacophony of tortured screams and maniacal laughter as Meridia scrambled back to her feet.

"She's here! She's here!" a woman's voice cackled from within one of the cells. Her demented elation echoed down the corridor, chasing Meridia as she hobbled as fast as she could towards her only way out.

A chorus of footsteps rang out behind her as a swarm of hooded figures poured into the hall and took up the chase, each one baying for her blood.

"Run Meridia, you're almost there..." the boy's voice returned, spurring her on.

As she picked up speed, the corridor began to crumble and shake, collapsing in on itself behind her. The hooded assailants began tumbling to their deaths, their harrowing screams composing a crescendo of chaos as the emerging chasm remained hot on Meridia's heels.

She was so close now and could feel the warmth from the amber light.

The intoxicating scent of hot chocolate and melted marshmallows flooded her nose to the point she could almost taste it.

Just as she got within arm's length of salvation, the ground beneath her gave way, and all Meridia could do was take one last leap of faith.

Down she fell into the darkness, plummeting for what felt like an eternity, until finally she landed on something soft and spongelike. Absorbing the full force of her impact, she sank momentarily, then gently sprung back up. Her entire body twitched in response to the rebound and the sensation was enough to wake her.

Meridia sat bolt upright, clambering for her breath as she frantically checked her surroundings. Her heart was galloping ten to the dozen as she tried to placate herself and look for evidence it had all been a dream. Sure enough, she was back in her bed, safe and sound. The hot chocolate her mother had made now looked cold, and sunlight was sneaking through the gap in her bedroom curtains. It was a brand-new day.

41

The next morning Kane awoke to Zach gently tapping on his door.

"What do you want?"

"It's 8:30 and we need to get ready."

"I'll be down in a minute," Kane replied curtly as he retreated under his duvet.

Following Peter's message, they all agreed to reconvene at 9am the next morning, giving themselves plenty of time to get to Crooked House for 10am.

Realizing his brother was right, Kane let out a deep sigh and acknowledged it was time to get up.

When he reached the kitchen, Zach was already crunching away on his third bowl of cereal. It was a typical Sunday in the Jackson household. Dad was in his man cave, most likely being brainwashed by the latest fitness hack in Men's Health, whilst mum was in the living room catching up on her soaps with a cup of coffee. It was another bright winter's day outside, one that Kane wanted to spend anywhere other than Crooked House.

Their last visit wasn't as successful as they'd first

thought, given the pandemic of shadow monsters trending when they got back. The fact nobody had been hurt, was the only slight consolation. There were some isolated incidents of bed-wetting, but as far as he knew, that was the worst of it.

When the doorbell rang a little before 9am, Kane and Zach were as ready as they could be.

They'd all agreed to tell their parents they were going to the park that day to avoid suspicion of all the sporting equipment they were carrying. Everyone was armed to the teeth with various clubs, bats, and rackets. As famous as Peter Higginsworth was, and as nice as he seemed on TV, they couldn't be too careful.

Ding dong!

"We're off to the park now, mum. Back before lunch!" Kane yelled as he grabbed his bag and set off with the gang in tow.

42

They were the first to arrive at Crooked House and they approached with trepidation.

There was a light, chilly breeze circling the house, which now looked even more run down since their last visit. The broken porch window didn't help matters, but it was more than that. Its fairy-tale mask was cracking to reveal the evil underneath.

Meridia found it even more uninviting now and questioned if she would have entered it at all if it looked that way yesterday.

"Is it me, or is this place falling apart by the day?" JJ asked.

"I was thinking exactly the same thing," Meridia concurred. "It looks much creepier today."

"You're just seeing it for what it is now, my dear," came the friendly, well-spoken voice behind them.

Peter Higginsworth stepped out from the dense woodland. He didn't fit the mould of a typical historian turned ghost hunter. Tall, athletic, and handsome, he had dirty blond hair that was greying at the temples of his chiselled face. He looked more like a movie star. Dressed in a casual blue sweater and black jeans, covered by a dressy wool overcoat, he leant on the tree next to him. His green eyes had a twinkle in them as he surveyed the group with a warm smile.

"Thank you for coming at such short notice guys," he stepped away from the tree and moved closer to the group.

As he did, Meridia caught a whiff of his cologne on the breeze and was instantly starstruck.

Kane was already in awe. He couldn't believe he was meeting one of his literary heroes.

"I'm sure you have hundreds of questions after yesterday, and I can't guarantee I'll be able to answer all of them, I'm afraid. Allow me to start by sharing my knowledge about this place, and we can assess the number of questions that are still unanswered at the end. Deal?"

The group nodded gormlessly. Peter mesmerized them, and so he began his story.

"Great! I'll keep this brief as possible, so I don't bore you all. I first came across Crooked House when I was researching for a book on haunted hotels. It had a local reputation for strange occurrences and ghostly sightings, so I came to visit one evening. The place didn't disappoint, and I ended up needing to dig deep into its history in order to better understand it. I decided not to publish everything I found at the time. I had my reasons, and with hindsight, that may not have been the best decision. We might not be here today if I'd just done more to warn people."

"What happened?" Zach interrupted.

"Shh," he said. "Questions at the end."

"Sorry, I forgot."

"It's ok ...Zach, isn't it? I guess the upshot of my experience was I took the place too lightly. If I had pushed a little harder with my editor or argued my case a little more with the owners, we might have saved more lives. A few years ago, I urged Helen to shut the place down, but she was so consumed with finding her husband Jonathan she just refused to listen. Now look at how everything has turned out..." Peter looked melancholy and lost in thought for a moment.

"Sorry, back to your question...I spent my first night at Crooked House on a warm summer's day in 2009. The only room they had available at the time was room 1, which was a little disappointing from my perspective, but the fan favourites were all booked months in advance, and I was working toward a tight deadline. Anyway, the owners were extremely hospitable and accommodating. It was clear from the outset it was Jonathan's baby. He had a boyish enthusiasm for the supernatural, which was infectious, and he always made sure guests left the B&B with some kind of tale to tell. It turned out he was an astute marketeer too. Helen on the other hand seemed to drift in and out, preferring to operate behind the scenes. Jonathan gave me a brief tour of the rooms and shared a smattering of the building's history, which he had embellished a little to help drum up business. I've been able to fill in several gaps since then, and the sad truth is neither of the owners knew quite what they had gotten themselves into when they bought the place. Crooked House has a violent and tragic history since it was built in the early 1700s. According to the rumours, the original owner murdered his wife one night in a fit of rage after discovering her in bed with another man. People say he was never apprehended, and rumour has it he still roams the halls at night, screaming his wife's name."

"Did you see him when you were there?" Zach couldn't

help himself at that point, and none of the others objected this time.

"Not quite, but now I believe what I saw was somehow connected to him. I'd spent much of the day wandering the building and grounds, taking photos and making audio recordings, but my initial encounter happened elsewhere in the house later that night. It was close to 10pm, and the day had been a bit of a dud until that point. Yes, I'd had the spiel from the owners and even spoken to a few other guests about their experiences, but I'd yet to see anything tangible so thought I'd retire for the night hoping to see something the following day. One thing I've learned from my travels is you can't force these things. Ghosts only ever show up when they want to. Anyway, I made my way out of the library and..."

"Wait, Crooked House has a library?" it was Izzy's turn to interrupt this time.

"Yes, it has a modest library-come-reading room for quests who want a bit of quiet. It's another marketing ploy, of course; full of books about ghosts and haunted houses. I noticed a few of my books when I was in there last, and there is, of course, the odd local history book thrown in too, although those were very basic. Anyway, as I walked toward my room, I passed the dining area, which had been closed down for the evening. The staff had neatly stacked all the tables and chairs in the dining area and covered them with dust sheets. It felt somewhat staged to me as the white sheets combined with the light from the outside porch gave the entire room an eerie quality. I saw something move out of the corner of my eye, so I looked inside. That's when I saw a dust sheet that was set apart from the rest and could see there was someone standing underneath it. Now I've been to enough haunted houses to expect the odd prank here and there, but this was different...it made the hairs on the back of my neck stand up. It was perfectly still. In the dim light, I could make out the contours of a face staring at me. I took a couple of steps to my right and approach it side-on, but as I moved away from its line of sight, the figure pivoted on the spot, watching me the entire time. I called out to whoever it was and told them I wasn't impressed, but the figure remained statuesque and unresponsive. The longer the creepy standoff continued, the more unsettling it became...it was quite intimidating, so eventually I reached for the light switch. The moment the lights came on, the dust sheet fell to the floor and whatever was underneath vanished right before my eyes! There was no way it could've been a hoax. I went over to the sheet and gave it a little kick; there were no wires attached to it, and nowhere for the culprit to hide afterward. But that wasn't the half of it. When I turned the light back off to continue to my room, standing in the shadows where the sheet had been, a creature appeared. It was shrouded in darkness, but I just knew it was what had been hiding under that dust sheet all along, staring me down. Its eyes glistened and sparkled in the shadows, and I found myself completely hypnotized by them...before I knew it, I felt paralyzed from the neck down. I just couldn't tear my eyes away from its gaze. The creature didn't move an inch, instead it whispered, 'we've been waiting for you, Peter,' and then evaporated into thin air. To this day, it still gives me the shivers whenever I think about it." Peter forced a smile, visibly shaken and distant, as if he'd relived every moment in the telling of his story.

The group was mesmerized by what they were hearing.

"They said they've been waiting for me, too." Zach mumbled.

"Chin up, young man. I haven't finished telling my story

yet. You've still to hear what happened when I got to my room that night."

"You still stayed? I'd have legged it home after what you saw." JJ's quip was for Zach's benefit more than anyone else, as he could see he was downcast.

"If it had been a little earlier in the day, I might have considered it. After what happened in the dining area, I went straight to my room without saying a word to anyone. When I got inside, the first thing I noticed was the temperature. It was a warm summer's evening outside, but room 1 felt more like the inside of a meat freezer. At the time, I wondered if Jonathan was putting on some kind of show for my benefit, so I searched around the room for any contraptions that could create such a chill. Despite what I had already seen, it's always important to stay vigilant. Alas I came up empty-handed, so I got ready for bed. I'd just finished brushing my teeth when I noticed a shadow behind me in the mirror. I turned and stepped back into my room to find that all the furniture, the walls, the fixtures, were all rapidly decomposing. Mould formed in the corners above the bed, spreading out and cracking the paintwork around the window frames. Dark brown stains formed on the red nylon rug, and a putrid stench like damp timber and rotten meat strangled the air. It was all I could do not to gag, so I had to get out of there. Just as I reached for the door, the words 'rot in hell' appeared in front of me. The message looked like someone had scrawled it in blood. I grasped the door handle and fled into the hallway, choking on the foul smell of death that filled my lungs. As I turned back, the room was perfectly normal, just as I'd found it. It was as if I'd imagined the whole thing."

"That sounds like what happened to us yesterday in the office. It was as if everything was drawn in crayon...it felt like we were trapped inside Jessica's mind or something," Kane blurted, connecting the dots while listening to Peter's story.

"That's exactly it Kane! You were...in a way, at least. I've learned, each room has its own unique way of interacting with the living, but they don't speak to just anybody. I reached out to countless guests and most claimed to see have seen shadowy figures lurking in the halls of this place during their stay, but none have communicated with them. None have experienced anything immersive in the rooms the way we have. Based on what I have learned over the years, that kind of ordeal seems to be reserved for a very select few, so welcome to the club."

"So who are they? The shadow monsters, I mean..." Meridia felt like they were finally getting some answers now and wanted to skip to the end.

"Well, if you google them now, you'll see sightings of shadow people happen all around the world and the phenomenon has been on a steady increase. There are hundreds of theories about who or what they are, but what I am about to tell you is the truth."

Peter paused a moment as he squatted on the edge of the grass in front of everyone. The group was now hanging on his every word.

"I know you're all still looking for answers, so I'll cut to the chase now and tell you why I brought you all here." He picked up a stick and used it to draw a golf ball sized circle in the dirt. "I want you to imagine this circle is our universe. Everyone and everything we know and understand lives within this circle. It's where we are right now. We'll call it 'Universe A' ok?"

Everyone nodded as Peter drew another circle next to it.

"This circle is another universe, let's call it 'Universe B'.

This one has some or all of us in it, but it's different. Maybe I'm a doctor in 'Universe B', or an astronaut, or maybe I haven't even been born. It follows the same basic laws as our universe, but its contents are slightly different to ours. Does that make sense?"

"You mean like a multiverse?" Izzy asked. The rest of the group looked at her in stunned silence. "What? I've been watching YouTube videos about quantum theory lately... and the Avengers collection on Disney."

"That's exactly it! Everything in 'Universe A' is already written, like fate. You were always going to find Crooked House, and we were always going to be back here today looking at circles in the dirt. We can't change the course we're all on here, but there are an ever-expanding number of other universes where things play out differently. Each universe is equally fixed in its own way, but each follows its own unique path to the next."

Peter then sketched a cluster of several more circles to illustrate his point and encompassed them with a larger circle.

"Let's call this bigger circle 'creation'. The more things that become possible, the more universes spawn inside of it, like multiplying cells in a petri dish. However, infinite possibilities present a bit of a capacity challenge over time, so creation self-regulates this by ensuring each universe doesn't just have a start point, but it also has an end point. It operates the same way all life does; people are born into the world just as people depart from it to make room. The circle of life, as they say. So, when a universe reaches its own unique end, it gets destroyed and taken over by our shadowy friends."

Peter took his stick and drew an s-shaped wavy line

from top to bottom, splitting the bigger circle into a yin and yang.

"You see? Light and dark. Life and death. Scientists now understand that energy never truly dies, it merely changes from one form to another. This is where it all goes."

Peter dropped the stick in the dirt and stood up tall.

"The shadow people you've seen are as old as time itself. They are known by several names, but they are most commonly referred to as the four horsemen and signify the onset of the apocalypse. There are currently three here in our universe at the moment. For those of you who aren't familiar with the New Testament, they are known as 'War', 'Famine' and 'Plague'. It's no coincidence reports of countries warring, unprecedented food shortages and outbreaks of new diseases increasingly dominated the news. Those are all symptoms of their growing influence over our world. They are preparing things for the arrival of the fourth horseman. He will signal the end of everything."

"What's so special about the fourth?" Zach couldn't resist jumping in.

"It's 'death'."

A chorus of gasps broke out amongst the group as the severity of their situation sank in.

"That's the one creature nobody has ever seen. It only arrives at the very end."

"At the end of what?"

"At the end of the prophecy Zach," Peter's tone became more serious, "The research I carried out uncovered an ancient prophecy that is said to signify the end of the world. Ten souls are taken on sacred ground as an offering to 'death'. When the tenth soul is taken, the world descends into darkness and night takes over."

Peter looked at Zach, who was still processing everything he'd heard.

"You are the tenth soul, Zach. That's why we're all here."

"That's what the monster meant when it said it had been waiting for you," Izzy blurted with her foot firmly in her mouth.

"Thanks Izzy," Zach replied, fighting back tears.

His sarcasm brought about a stunned silence, as everyone realized their insensitivity. Truth was they had been so caught up in Peter's revelations that despite their questions, they had somehow disassociated themselves from the implications.

All except Zach, that was.

For all the talk of death, and lost souls had left him reeling and fearful for his life. The foreboding words of his own 'echo' slinked around in his overwhelmed mind, infecting his every thought with its ominous tone.

Zach believed his fate was now sealed, and everyone he loved faced inevitable doom.

"Hey, it's ok Zach," Peter continued, putting an end to the uncomfortable hush that had befell the group. "I've found you first. I think we can stop them this time."

"What do you mean 'this time?'" Kane probed.

"The shadow people are limited to the souls they can take. I had a chance to stop them before, but I got there too late. I blew it..." Peter hung his head and stared solemnly at the circles in the dirt.

"Jessica?" Asked Meridia. Peter closed his eyes and shook his head.

"There was a boy...a very bright and brilliant boy...he was a similar age to all of you actually...about fifteen, I believe...he had his entire future ahead of him. His name was Archie."

43

The rain had been hammering the village of Thundridge for three whole days now. Sheet upon sheet poured down relentlessly from the silvery sky, flooding the gutters, and clogging the fields.

Archie listened to its dreary thrum hitting his window as he watched the alarm clock next to his bed approach 7:00am. It was the first day of half-term. He'd been awake for about an hour now, watching and listening, but found the warm, cozy embrace of his duvet too good to leave.

The alarm finally sounded, and it was time to get up. Tapping the silence button, he threw his covers down toward his feet, swinging his legs out of bed. His coarse, dirty blonde hair looked like an explosion in a mattress factory, whilst his hazel eyes sparkled in the morning sun creeping in through the gap in his curtains. For weeks, he had been waiting for this day to come.

"Payday!" he announced, springing into action, grabbing yesterday's joggers and hoodie from the floor next to him.

Archie Faulkner had been doing his paper round since

the day he turned fifteen and this was his third payday. The round was tiny and only included a handful of customers, so his earnings were modest, but it was one of the few ways he could earn money at his age.

This week's wage meant he would have enough money to buy something from the local second-hand bookstall in town, and he knew exactly what that was going to be. He'd been window shopping there religiously every Saturday, and eying up a copy of *Poe's Complete Works*.

Archie was an avid horror reader and aspiring poet, so Poe was a literary hero of his. Each week, he visited the stall and made sure the precious book was tucked safely at the bottom of the pile before he left. Today was the day he would finally buy it.

Opening his curtains, he smelt his armpits and then grabbed the roll-on next to his bed. "*Good to go,*" he said to himself, as he wandered down the hall to wake his sister. "Time to get up, Princess Peach," he whispered while tapping the door.

In a matter of seconds, the door opened and Katie emerged.

She was half the height of her brother but shared the same coarse hair, which looked as if she'd been dragged through a hedge backwards. Archie doted on his sister, and it never ceased to amaze him how adorable she was first thing in the morning. She let out a cute little half-yawn, grabbing him by the hand.

"What's for breakfast?" she whispered.

"Coco flakes today, madam. How would you like them?" Both siblings continued to keep their voices low while they wandered past their father's bedroom. His door was closed, as it often was these days.

"In my princess bowl...please."

"Why certainly, madam." Archie hoisted his sister up onto his back and gingerly walked downstairs to the kitchen.

The Faulkners had fallen on hard times of late and their dad was struggling to find his feet again. He'd often come home from a day of looking for work, only having found a six-pack of cheap beer at the local convenience store. He would then spend the evening drinking himself into a stupor before crashing out on the sofa in front of the tv.

It had been that way for the better part of a year now, ever since they had lost their mum suddenly to cancer.

Archie could hardly remember what life had been like before she passed. It felt like a murky dream, shrouded in fog and sorrow.

He placed three bowls on the kitchen counter, filling each with cereal, and then added milk to two of them. Slurping and crunching, they both devoured their breakfast as if it was their first meal in a week.

"Movie time," Archie announced, and Katie responded as she always did.

Facing him, she placed each of her feet on top of her brother's, held his hands and then insisted he proceed to the lounge, walking like Frankenstein's monster.

"Again!" she beamed with glee when they reached the brown leather chesterfield closest to the tv.

Archie accommodated by doing a lap of honour around the room whilst his pint-sized passenger showered him with fits of giggles.

"I've just got to wash up and then I'll be on my way. Dad is upstairs though, so wake him up if you need anything, and don't answer the front door if anyone knocks, ok?"

Katie nodded robotically, half-listening to her brother as she surveyed the selection of kids' movies on offer.

Archie gave his sister a light kiss goodbye on the top of her head and returned to the kitchen. As expected, the bin was overflowing with empty beer cans, so he put two heaping spoonfuls of instant coffee in a mug and filled the kettle up with fresh water.

The weather was still dire when he glanced outside, so Archie grabbed his waterproof jacket and left via the backdoor.

"Back soon," he called, a little louder than usual, in the hope it might give his dad a nudge upstairs. Katie didn't answer; no doubt she was fully engrossed in her movie now. He closed the door behind him and set off for work.

When Archie arrived at Fourboys Newsagents, he was already soaked. The rain hadn't let up, and he'd been riding headlong into it the entire way there.

Mr Turner gave him his usual warm greeting when he arrived and handed him a high-vis orange bag with a tattered and grubby white nylon strap. Inside were a handful of newspapers, along with a carton of orange juice, which he always threw in for good measure. He was a kind old man who, with the help of his wife, had run the local newsagents for the last thirty years. He'd seen a great deal of change during that time and what was once a thriving local shop, now barely ticked over.

"I'll have your wage for you when you get back, Archie. Be careful out there. The roads will be slippery."

"Thanks Mr Turner, will do and I'll be back soon."

Despite the awful weather, Archie relished any

opportunity to ride his bike. Even though it was an old BMX and felt a little small for him, it was one of the few nice things his dad had done since it had been just the three of them. It was built for stunts with its chrome mongoose frame, red mushroom grips, matching tires, and trick nuts at the rear.

On dry days, Archie would spend hours in his drive practicing moves he'd seen on tv and building ramps from old bits of wood. However, today it would be all business as he was desperate to get to the book stall. His personal best for finishing his round was twenty minutes flat, but that was on a dry day, so he figured he'd settle for a respectable thirty today.

The last thing his dad or Katie needed was for Archie to get hurt.

And with that sobering thought, he set off.

44

Having completed his round and returned Mr Turner's orange bag, Archie hightailed it to the bookstall. He felt the envelope of cash burning a hole in his pocket as he frantically peddled all the way there.

The stall was already set up when he pulled up to the old concrete bookstand as customers ferreted through the many books on offer.

Mrs Chen, the owner, sat at her makeshift table reading her own book, ready to offer recommendations if asked. She was a local woman, somewhere in her mid-forties. Her husband was the town GP, and she saw the book stall as a rewarding passion project to occupy her time whilst he was at work.

"Hey Archie, what are you doing out so early? You look soaked." Mrs Chen was a bookworm and loved Archie's enthusiasm for classic literature. In her experience, he was a rare breed, with so many kids his age preferring to bury themselves in a video game rather than a novel.

"I just finished my round for the week and it's payday."

Archie flashed a toothy grin from beneath his hood as

he hurried over to the box labelled 'P'. He lifted the pile and pulled out the tiny coral book that was still where he'd left it.

"I'll take this one please, Mrs Chen."

"Ah, a good choice, but is it not scary for you?" she quizzed.

"I've been dying to buy this book for weeks; he's my favourite author. I love reading anything dark and creepy." Archie could barely contain his excitement as he handed over his hard earned money for the book.

"You're very brave. But what about real ghosts? I've got another book here somewhere that you might like..."

Mrs Chen stood up and wandered over to the box labelled 'H'. She riffled through the contents and then smiled as she pulled a worn black paperback from the pile.

"It's ok Mrs Chen, I can only afford the one this time," Archie said with a tinge of embarrassment.

"Nonsense, you can have this one, on the house. Consider it buy one, get one free today, I insist." She said, handing it over to him.

"*Britain's Most Haunted Hotels*...wow thanks; that's really kind. Peter Higginsworth...I've not heard of him before." Archie flipped the book around to read the blurb on the back.

> *Join renowned paranormal expert Peter Higginsworth as he travels the country in search of Britain's most haunted hotels. This is your definitive guide to the supernatural, featuring over 30 individual stories of haunted hotels, creepy castles, and eerie inns around the UK. Full to the brim with genuine, real-life scares, including multiple interviews and eyewitness accounts, this book will convert even the most hardened of sceptics! Read it if you dare...*

"A stranger donated it earlier this week, but I don't sell many non-fiction. I had a quick flick through the hotels and there is one that's not too far from here. I hope you enjoy it."

Archie's eyes lit up at the prospect of a nearby haunting and couldn't wait to get home and start reading it. He thanked Mrs Chen again as he jumped back on his bike and set off towards home.

When Archie returned home, his dad was sitting at the kitchen table hugging a cup of coffee and staring into space.

He looked haggard, as if he'd aged ten years in as many months. Grey temples had inched their way down his narrow jawline, framing his solemn expression with patchy white stubble. The nurses were concerned with his rapid weight loss at the time Archie's mum got sick. He dropped a couple of inches around his waist almost overnight and now, no matter how much food he ate, or beer he guzzled, the weight refused to return. 'Nervous energy', the palliative nurse had called it at the time. It remained a telltale sign there was still more going on behind his glazed blue eyes than he was currently able to process.

"Hey dad, you ok?" Archie nudged him from his trance as he walked to the fridge. He placed the carton of orange juice Mr Turner had given him earlier inside and closed the door. Archie didn't care much for fruit juice, but Katie loved it, so he always saved them for her.

"Hi...sorry...I didn't hear you come in. Thanks for the coffee. I need to go into town today, so are you ok to stay home with your sister?"

"Of course. I've got a couple of new books to read, so was planning on staying in anyway."

"Thanks...there are some pizzas in the freezer, so just eat without me later. I'll sort myself out when I get back." His brow was furrowed, almost buckling under the weight of the world that sat heavily on his shoulders.

Archie felt at a complete loss, watching him wander out of the front door like a zombie. He kept telling himself the dark cloud looming over his dad would pass, but just like the inclement weather bludgeoning his village, there was no sign of any let up.

Once he'd heard the street door close, Archie made his way upstairs to check on Katie before settling down on his bed to read.

Three hours had passed by the time Katie tapped on Archie's door.

"I'm hungry," she said, peering round the door frame. "What's for lunch?" Archie looked at his clock and couldn't believe how much time had passed. He'd been totally absorbed in the book Mrs Chen had gifted him, particularly the section relating to Crooked House.

"Sorry madam, I didn't realize the time. What would you like?"

"Peanut butter and jam, please!"

"Crunchy or smooth?" Archie teased.

"Crunchy silly! I'm a big girl now, remember?" Katie was grinning and fidgeting with excitement, ready to break into a jig.

She enjoyed her food and was a good eater, always open to trying whatever new concoctions her brother whipped up when their dad was out. She'd stuck on peanut butter and jam, though, particularly when she graduated to the crunchy kind.

"Ok, let's go!" Archie swept her up under his arm and then carried her downstairs to the kitchen.

After demolishing lunch, Archie stayed in the living room with Katie while she watched another movie. He figured it would give him the chance to do some research on his phone without neglecting her.

Fascinated by what he'd just read, and the fact a genuine haunted hotel was nearby, he was desperate to know more. When he searched his map, he found Crooked House was a mere forty-minute walk, which meant he could make it there in under thirty on his bike. Archie clicked the website link and his heart sank a little when it connected him to the home page.

It is with a heavy heart that I must announce Crooked House has now permanently closed its doors to the public. The team and I would like to thank you for all the wonderful memories and support you've given us over the years, and we hope to see you again one day.

Happy hauntings.
- Helen

45

Undeterred, Archie ran a wider search and found several reviews and articles on the many haunted rooms of Crooked House. He hopped from link to link, feverishly assimilating anything he could find. Stories of shadowy figures prowling the halls, murderous husbands and ghosts from WW2 fed his fixation as he lost himself further and further down the rabbit hole.

Archie didn't even notice when Katie's movie finished, or when she retreated upstairs to her room; he was too busy reading about the owner's mysterious disappearance, along with that of a girl named Jessica.

Just when he felt like he'd exhausted all there was on the subject, he came across an enigmatic blogger named '*Retiarius*'.

His articles and comments seemed more than a little neurotic, but boasted a deep understanding of Crooked House and Cold Christmas, both from a personal and historical perspective. As Archie continued to read, the blog took on a darker tone, talking in detail about devil worship, initiation ceremonies and missing children dating back centuries.

The common theme of all Retiarius' ramblings was simple: *stay away*.

As he sat over pizza, Archie couldn't help but think about Crooked House and how much he wanted to see it firsthand. He figured he would cycle there the following morning if his dad was home to look after Katie, and so decided he would ask when he eventually came home that evening. His dad was pretty agreeable when he had a couple of beers in him, and as much as Archie felt guilty for asking to go out, he guessed he could be there and back within a couple of hours.

"Can we play now?" Katie had scoffed her pizza and was staring expectantly at Archie from across the kitchen table. Over the last few months, they had developed an evening routine of playing card games together, followed by a bedtime story.

Because of their age gap, the card games all revolved around cartoon animals and relied heavily on memory, but Archie enjoyed it all the same and was always pleasantly surprised when Katie gave him a run for his money. Archie won three games to two, which felt like a win for Katie.

By the time he had finished reading that evening, Katie was sound asleep and cuddled up to her favourite toy; a soft grey rabbit she'd named 'Bit'. Archie wondered how much of all this Katie would remember when she got older. His own memory of being five was non-existent, which meant there was every chance she'd forget about their mum altogether.

A tiny knot formed in his throat, making it hard to breathe for a moment, and he felt the onset of tears threatening to flood his eyes. He took in a deep breath and regained control before swallowing the knot back down into the depths of his stomach.

A shadow passed by in the hall and Archie became acutely aware of someone else's presence in the house. He hadn't heard the front door open or close, so he thought maybe it was his mind playing tricks after all his reading.

Creeping out into the hall, he pulled Katie's door closed and whispered,

"Dad? Dad, is that you?"

When he didn't get an answer, Archie ventured downstairs to investigate. The second stair from the bottom had a weak panel and always creaked whenever anyone stepped on it. Standing outside his dad's empty room, Archie heard its familiar groan.

"Dad? Are you home?" he called a little louder from the top step, but there was still no reply.

He had no choice now but go down. When he reached the downstairs hallway, he saw another shadow dancing back and forth in the kitchen. He was certain he'd turned that light off after dinner, just as he always did.

A slight shiver made its way under the bottom of Archie's untucked t-shirt and tip-toed up his back as he questioned if he'd locked the back door. By the time he had reached the kitchen, he had convinced himself Retiarius had somehow tracked his IP address and broken in to murder him and his sister in their beds.

Flush with fear, Archie took a couple of shallow breaths to steady himself before holding a deeper one in as he looked around the corner. When he saw his dad slumped over the table, beer can in hand, he immediately let out a tremendous sigh of relief.

"Dad? Are you ok?" he called, gently placing a hand on his shoulder.

"I'm sorry Arch...I...I saw you reading to Katie and wanted to come in...I wanted to throw my arms around you both and tell you how sorry I am...and how much I love you...but I...something just stops me...you both look so much like her, and then it all comes crashing down on me. I...I'm trying Arch...I'm trying so hard!" His dad slumped back over the table again and began so sob.

Archie felt the knot return to his throat, so he buried his face in his dad's back with a hug and cried with him.

He hoped he was witnessing the beginning of a breakthrough rather than a breakdown. As sad as it was, his dad had been bottling his emotions up for so long it was reassuring to know he was still in there somewhere fighting to get out.

"I know it's hard, dad. It's hard for all of us...but we'll get through this. We have to."

"Your mum was always better at this than me. She always knew what to do...she'd be so proud if she could see you...I just don't know what to do anymore. I'm so sorry..."

"It's ok dad. Everyone knows you're doing your best. Why don't you get some rest, yeah?"

Archie helped his weary father out of the chair and guided him up to his room. There was little resistance, and he fell asleep as soon as his head hit the pillow. The room was fraught with the smell of stale beer, so Archie opened one of the windows a little and then quietly turned in for the night, too.

46

The next morning, Archie awoke to the smell of toast and fried bacon. When he threw on his clothes and left his room, both Katie's and his dad's bedrooms were empty, so he wandered down to the kitchen.

"Hey Arch, perfect timing. I was just about to send your sister up to wake you."

His dad was clumsily buttering toast while a jug of eggs were busy being scrambled by the microwave. Meanwhile, Katie was loitering around the fridge, eyeing up the pile of bacon resting on the middle of the table.

"I thought I'd cook breakfast for a change so we could all eat together. Hope that's ok?"

"That's...awesome, and it beats coco flakes."

"What are you up to today? I thought you might want to go out and ride your bike or climb trees...or do whatever it is you and your mates get up to these days."

Archie could tell his dad was trying really hard, and this level of effort was way outside of his comfort zone, but the gesture alone filled Archie with hope. If he hadn't known better, he'd have half-expected his mum to appear, offering to pour everyone orange juice. The tiny crack in Archie's heart, the one he'd carried all year alone, spread just a fraction at the thought of his mum not being there. These were the moments that made her absence all too real again, as if they'd only just lost her.

"Thanks dad. I think I'll go for a ride in that case. I won't be too long though, I promise."

After they'd all eaten, and he had reminded his dad how to access the kids' movies on their tv, Archie set off in search of ghosts.

As HE APPROACHED the gravel road leading to Crooked House, Archie realized how secluded it was, and how isolated that made him. The path he needed to follow veered off towards a dense wooded area, and something deep inside was niggling at him to pay more attention to his surroundings.

Despite the onslaught of rain, it had been a relatively mild October, and the gently swaying golden leaves danced in the breeze as they defiantly clung onto their branches, refusing to accept the onset of autumn. Those that had succumbed, languished below in a muculent slew of dirty brown remnants, obscuring the grassy bank that lay hidden beneath.

Archie checked his phone signal before going any further, only to find the dreaded message of '*No Network Available*' staring back at him. The realization he was now alone caused Retiarius' foreboding stories to all come flooding back, and he wondered how much truth was in them.

"I can't go back yet," he mumbled as he peddled his bike over the shingly track towards the house.

When he arrived at the clearing outside, the wind whipped up a notch, setting an old rocking chair in motion that was on the front porch. It was a quaint-looking building and far smaller than Archie had imagined.

"Think hotel is a bit of a stretch Peter." he quipped as he set his bike down to take a closer look.

When he approached the front door, the wind quietened and an eerie silence befell the grounds, as if time had somehow frozen still. The glass was smeared with grease and grime, which made it nigh on impossible to see anything inside. The whole place looked shrouded in darkness despite its many windows, so Archie presumed all the doors had been closed, perhaps to lock the ghosts in.

He cupped his hands around his face and pressed his nose to the glass, but all he could make out was the vague rectangular outline of a sofa or table. Still pressed against the window and squinting, he heard a twig snap behind him.

Crooked House had another visitor.

"What are you doing?" Archie leapt in fright at the unexpected voice, as his legs involuntarily gave out underneath him.

The result sent him toppling backwards off the porch and onto the ground with a thump.

"Are you ok? I didn't mean to scare you." Archie looked up to find a girl standing over him with a troubled expression etched across face.

His first thought was how captivating she was, with large blue eyes and a thick blonde bob which hovered around her jawline, accentuating her perfect cheekbones. Archie was immediately smitten by her entire look; ripped blue denim jeans and a marled grey hoodie with a smart black leather jacket on top.

"Wow...er...ahem....who...who are you?"

The girl stretched out a well-manicured hand sporting shiny black almond nails to help him up.

"I'm Georgia. What are you doing here?"

Archie kept his head down while he dusted himself off; he could feel his cheeks burning with embarrassment.

"I'm Archie...I read about this place in a book and came to look around. I heard that it's haunted."

Having gathered his composure, he looked up to find the girl had left him talking to the trees. Georgia walked to the front door and tried to see inside.

"You're wasting your time...it's too dark. What are you doing here?" Georgia conceded and turned to face him.

Archie guessed she might be a couple of years old than him, and almost as tall. He then realized he may have been staring at her a little too intensely and so reunited his gaze with the ground whilst she pondered his question.

"I'm looking for someone...they're missing, and I know this place is connected somehow. I need to find a way inside." Georgia dabbed her eyes with the cuff of her jacket as she rushed to the largest window at the font of the house and inspected it.

"Er, I'm not sure that's a good idea. The things I read about this place...if even half of them are true..."

"You're not scared, are you? Why come here if you're scared?" Georgia was buzzing around, cupping her hands at windows in search of a way in.

Archie didn't rise to the bait, "I just wanted to see it. I've never seen a haunted house before, and this place is meant to be as haunted as they come."

"Do you believe a place can be evil, Archie? I don't

mean the people in it; I mean the actual place; the bricks and mortar."

"I don't know. I guess bricks and mortar were put together by someone, so surely it all traces back to people. Like the history of this place. It's all just people."

"I stayed here once as a kid. The stories...they're all true. It's evil, Archie...this place. Don't let it fool you. Too many bad things have happened here for too long. I came here looking for answers. I was gonna storm right in there and get them, but when I got here...I dunno...I'd been circling this place for an hour before you got here, trying to come up with a plan, but now I'm here I'm too bloody scared to go in on my own."

Archie could see the war raging behind Georgia's eyes.

Half of her wanted to kick the door down, whilst the other half wanted to run for the hills.

"Who is it? The person you're trying to find?"

"My dad...he's been gone a long time, but I just thought if I came here...I might find out what really happened to him."

"I'm sorry. I lost my mum almost a year ago now. My dad's still finding it hard...I guess we all are in our own way."

"I just want to know what happened to him; you know? There are files in there; one for every room."

"Who told you that?" Archie was intrigued as he thought he'd exhausted all the intel on Crooked House, uncovering even the wildest conspiracy theories attached to it, but there was no mention of any files.

"I've seen them. My dad used to own this place. They were his files."

"Wait...does that mean your dad is...er..."

"Jonathan Ashfield. His wife Helen is my step-mum.

When she closed this place, I thought I'd finally get some answers, but she won't return any of my calls, she won't even answer her door to me...and so, here I am."

Georgia shrugged her shoulders in resignation of the fact she didn't have much of a plan beyond turning up. The house was securely locked, and breaking a window seemed to be the only option.

"What would you do if you were me, Archie? What would you do if it was your mum? You'd go in there, right? So why am I so chicken shit now I'm here?"

"You're right, I'd do the same. I don't blame you for being scared though; this place has a pretty bad rep, even if you don't believe in all the ghost stories. The last thing you want to do is end up in trouble."

Archie could almost hear the cogs whirring inside Georgia's mind as she weighed up her options.

"Listen, I wanna help, but I have to get back home soon. I need to check in on my dad and there's no signal here. Do you live nearby? How did you even get here?"

Archie became aware there was no sign of a car or bike around them.

"I'm visiting my aunt and uncle in Cold Christmas. Their place is about a ten-minute walk from here. I'm only staying with them for a few more days and then I'll be getting the train back home. I have to get inside."

"Ok, well, how about I meet you back here in a day or two? I'll bring some torches and in the meantime, we can both have a think about how we get inside without getting ourselves arrested. Deal?"

"Really? You'd do that for me?" It was Georgia's turn to blush, but the reality was Archie would have said yes to pretty much anything she asked of him.

"How about Wednesday, 10am? That gives us a couple of days to come up with a plan."

Georgia paced the porch for a second while she considered Archie's offer.

"OK, it's a date. Shall I give you my number then, just in case you decide to cancel on me?"

Archie was bad at picking up signals from the opposite sex, but he could have sworn he was being flirted with.

"Of course, but I'll be here, I promise."

Archie handed Georgia his phone and with a flurry of tapping, she entered her number.

"Thanks. I'd better go, so I'll message when I get home and see you here Wednesday."

"Cool. I'll see you then."

47

Archie made it back home in record time; there was a fresh wind in his sails and her name was Georgia Ashfield. Not only had he seen a haunted hotel that day, but he'd also met a real-life damsel in distress; one he was determined to help.

He propped his bike up against the garden fence and pulled his phone out.

> Hey Georgia, this is Archie.
> Great to meet u and I'll c u
> Wednesday.

A warm smile radiated across Archie's face at the thought of seeing her again. It had been a long time since he'd seen anyone outside of school and he was worried he was retreating into his shell a little of late.

Despite the less-than-ideal circumstance, Archie embraced his romantic nature and believed in fate. He wondered what the chances were of both he and Georgia visiting Crooked House at exactly the same time that day. There had to be a reason.

Archie felt his phone vibrate in his pocket.

A message from Georgia.

```
Great to meet u 2. See u
wed x.
```

Archie noticed the thick, musty smell of beer when he entered the kitchen through the back door. The familiar scent made his stomach churn and heart plummet into a deep, dark well of disappointment.

"Dad? Katie?"

He trudged towards the living room expecting to find his dad asleep on the sofa and Katie sat in front of the tv, but the room was empty.

"Dad?"

Approaching the bottom of the stairs, he heard Katie's infectious giggle, followed by his dad's laughter. It was a sound Archie had almost forgotten, but his reacquaintance with it triggered an immense wave of relief, washing away the worry of any potential relapse.

Peering around Katie's door, he saw she had all her favourite dolls laid out, and they were both busy styling their hair in wacky outlandish ways.

They were clearly having a great time, as his dad's fingernails on his left hand were painted a variety of colours. It was a joy to see, and long overdue, so Archie quietly carried on down the hallway towards his room so as not to disturb them. Katie needed her dad, and for the first time all year, she actually had him.

Once in his room, the only thing on Archie's mind were the files Georgia had mentioned at Crooked House so he quickly resumed his research online. Having bookmarked all the useful websites he'd found the previous day, it was easy to pick up right where he'd left off, but he found no mention of them anywhere.

The constant juggling of tiny articles on his phone soon aggravated him, so Archie reached underneath his bed and pulled out an A1 sketch pad. He often used this to storyboard his own stories and poems, so figured it would be a good idea to do the same with what he knew about Crooked House. By the time he was finished, it was less storyboard and more murder board.

The number of connections astonished him though, and the more he put together, the more weight it gave to Georgia's theory that the building itself was evil. There had been a long history of tragedy in the area, dating all the way back to the 18th Century when the territory was the focus of the Witch-finder General and his men.

Since then, an unusually high number of children had been reported either missing or presumed dead; with one large spike occurring in the early forties, followed by another in the seventies. Among them, there were also a few adults, including Georgia's dad, who the authorities had recently declared dead, even though they never found his body.

Along with Crooked House, it seemed Cold Christmas also had a shady past, and the sleepy village used to be home to the scourge of society, harbouring a myriad of criminals from petty thieves to murderers and everything in between. Still, there wasn't a sniff of the files Georgia had mentioned and Archie had explored every avenue available to him.

Or had he?

Archie wrote at the top of his page '*Peter Higginsworth?*' and then searched for him online. It wasn't long before he found his social media pages and so Archie decided to reach out and make contact. Peter had investigated various locations, and his feed was littered with them, including a haunted clock tower in North London. With time being in short supply, Archie concluded his best bet would be a direct message, hoping to prompt a quick response.

Hi Peter, I need to talk to you about Crooked House. I was there earlier today and think I've found something which will interest you.

Archie reread his message and hit send.

It was a longshot, and he didn't expect any reply, but he had to try for Georgia.

"Hey Arch, I didn't hear you come in." his dad was standing in the doorway with Katie.

They were both grinning like Cheshire cats.

"Hey guys. I didn't want to interrupt earlier; you both looked like you were having so much fun." Archie subtly shut his pad and gave his dad his full attention. "I just thought I'd catch up on some schoolwork."

"That's a good idea; get it out of the way early and enjoy the rest of your week off. I'll be cooking dinner soon, so I'll give you a shout when it's ready. Meanwhile, Princess Peach and I have a date with Rhonda and the Forbidden Kingdom on tv. Come on darling."

And with that, they both wandered out of sight.

Only a couple of seconds had passed before Katie came bounding back in and jumped up on Archie's bed. She clasped both arms around his neck and blew a big raspberry on his cheek, then toddled out again. Archie felt tears welling up for a moment.

For the first time in forever, he felt full of hope that they could find their way back to being a family again.

Before his mind could explore that notion further, he heard a short, sharp buzz from his bedside table.

Peter Higginsworth had replied to his message.

48

Thank you for your message. Crooked House remains of great interest to me, but please do not underestimate how dangerous it is, particularly at night. I would strongly recommend you avoid the place at all costs. I am on a ghost hunt right now but will be free to speak on this number around 8pm this evening if you are happy to talk?
  Best
  PH

Archie couldn't believe he'd had a response, let alone one so quickly. He'd never spoken to a celebrity before and suddenly felt a little nervous but agreed to make the call.

When the clock turned 8pm Archie was already in his room, headphones in and waiting for Peter's call. The phone rang not a minute later.

"Hello?"

"Hi, Archie, isn't it?"

Peter was well spoken, and his voice had an air of equanimity about it.

"So, tell me, what were you doing at Crooked House?"

Archie told Peter his story, from being gifted his book and how that sparked his own minor research project, to then eventually winding up visiting the place that morning. Peter showed great interest, not just in what Archie had learned about Crooked House, but also in Archie himself. He seemed encouraging about his writing and even offered to read some of his poems.

After an hour or so, it felt more like they were old friends shooting the breeze, as Peter shared stories from the haunted location he was studying in London. Eventually Archie felt comfortable enough to mention the files Georgia had told him about and Peter went quiet for the first time since their call had started.

"Who told you about the files, Archie?"

There was a seriousness in Peter's tone that Archie hadn't heard until now, so he figured he would keep Georgia's identity a secret for the moment.

"There was a girl there when I arrived. She didn't stay long, so I'm not sure if I scared her off, but she told me about them. She said the place itself is evil, that it was way more than a haunted hotel."

Peter took another long pause at his end of the line.

"There are files, Archie. I recommended the owner keep them after I visited the place; to document strange activity in each room. The girl you met today. What did she look like?"

"She was a little older than me...blonde...tall for a girl, I guess. She didn't stick around long, though."

"Did you notice anything unusual about her? Did you see what colour her eyes were?"

Archie felt that was an odd question, but decided it was safe to answer honestly.

"They were blue...her eyes. There wasn't anything strange about her, though. She seemed normal, just scared."

"She's right to be scared, and so should you be. There is an evil in that place, lurking in the shadows. It's unlike anything I've ever come up against; a monster who steals the souls of the living. Each of its victims end up trapped there, vanished from the outside world and imprisoned in the rooms of Crooked House. I've seen them with my own eyes, Archie, and some are not to be trifled with. Each has a strange power or unique way of interacting with the world of the living. I don't understand how or why, yet, but I've been following it from afar for years now and it's getting stronger with every soul it takes. I fear that's why Helen has been forced to close it down. The files you mentioned, there are eight of them, and they contain everything known about each room. My theory is whatever dark forces are at play in Crooked House they are trying to fill each room with one of their victims, which means we're running out of time. I'm worried about the girl you met today, Archie. I'm worried she could be in grave danger."

Archie felt a strong sense of dread engulf him, and he squirmed uncomfortably on the edge of his bed. If what Peter was saying was true, then Georgia might be in real danger. He had to warn her.

"Archie!"

"I need to go, Peter. My dad needs me downstairs."

"I know this all sounds crazy, Archie, and you don't know me from Adam, but trust me when I say Crooked House is very dangerous. Maybe more than ever since its closure. Stay away from it, and if you see the girl again, tell her the same thing. You might just save her life. I'm here if you need me, Archie. I mean that."

"Thanks Peter. I'll be in touch if anything else comes up."

And with that, Archie ended the call and trotted downstairs. When he entered the living room, he found his dad bent over the tv as if he'd lost something down the back of the unit.

"What's up, dad?"

"Ah, there you are. I can't find the right socket for the old camcorder. I promised to show Katie the wedding video in the morning but can't plug the damn thing in!"

Perplexed, his dad handed him the cable, then turned red with embarrassment when Archie solved the problem in a matter of seconds.

"Thanks Arch...god that made me feel old!" His dad gave him a wry smile as he rubbed his jawline in contemplation.

"Are you sure you're up to watching that stuff?" he clumsily probed.

"I can't keep pretending she didn't exist, son...I owe her more than that. I owe both you kids more than that, too. It'll be good for Katie...and me, I think. I'll be fine...I promise."

"As long as you're sure. There's no need to rush anything...I'm going to call it a night I think dad...maybe read a little in bed. You sure you're ok?" Archie tried to get a better read on his father, tempering any hopes that he may have finally turned a corner.

"I'm fine...honest. You go up, and I expect I won't be too far behind."

He gave Archie a warm reassuring smile. One that he hadn't seen in a long time, and as he left his dad in the living room fumbling with old video cassettes, Archie allowed himself to believe there might be a light at the end of the tunnel.

Feeling buoyant when he reached his room, he remembered he still hadn't updated Georgia on his conversation with Peter, so he slumped onto his bed and hastily pulled his phone from his pocket.

```
Hey, hope ur ok. I've been
warned about Crooked House by
the author of that book. He
said it's evil, and we could
be in danger if we go back x
```

He paused for a moment, questioning if he should add the kiss, then accidentally clipped the send button with his thumb as it hovered above his screen in hesitation.

A rush of blood flooded his cheeks for the umpteenth time that day.

"What is it about his girl?" he muttered to himself and then got ready for bed.

49

The next morning, Archie awoke to find the rain had returned. He felt punch drunk from a terrible night's sleep, which he attributed to his overactive imagination. Although he rarely remembered his dreams the next day, he was left with a lingering feeling he'd spent most of the night scared.

He checked his phone and found he had two messages, one from Georgia and another from Peter.

The kiss he'd accidentally sent on purpose came flooding back to him and turned his stomach into a butterfly reserve.

> Hey Archie, I thought u promised u wouldn't cancel? Do you trust this author? What if he's the one behind it all? If u don't want to come that's fine and I'll just go it alone. I need 2 know what happened to my dad xx

Archie felt a mix of emotions as he read it. He sensed a

pang of guilt over his sudden u-turn, as if he'd let Georgia down, but by the same token, he couldn't stop counting the number of kisses at the end of her message.

"Get a grip man," he said to himself as he typed his reply.

```
Don't want to let u down, but
he said u could be in danger
if u go inside. I don't want
anything to happen to u xx.
```

He figured it was safe to match her kiss quota for the moment, so he hit send. The second his message left, he began wondering if her double kiss was in fact a typo and if he'd just crossed a line.

"Honestly, Archie, it's just a message."

She made a fair point about Peter, though. As much as Archie trusted him on the call last night, he didn't know anything about him and, for all he knew, he might be a serial killer. But if Peter's motives were sinister, then why would he warn them away?

He decided to read his message.

Hi Archie, just wanted to thank you again for reaching out yesterday; it was the right thing to do and aside from the serious nature of our call, I enjoyed our chat. Anyway, I hope you can move on to more positive things now, like your writing, and put that wretched place behind you.

I meant what I said yesterday; I'd love to see some of your work, so feel free to send me whatever you're comfortable with and if there's anything I can do to help, then I will.

All the best
PH

It was a sweet message and Archie had lots of samples he could send him. He'd never shared his work with anyone before, and the thought of sending something to a published author felt daunting.

Before giving the matter anymore thought, his phone buzzed with a new message from Georgia.

```
That's sweet, but I'm a big
girl. I'm heading there now to
find a way in. I read there's
a board around the back so
hoping I can loosen it. I'll
let you know what happens, but
if you don't hear from me
again, then it was lovely to
meet u xxx
```

"Shit!"

Archie had to stop her somehow.

He threw his clothes on and almost collided with Katie as he flew out of his bedroom door.

"Woah, sorry Princess. I didn't see you there. Are you ok?"

Startled, Katie's bottom lip quivered as she teetered on the brink of tears.

"Hey, it's ok, I was just in a rush. I need to help a friend."

Archie picked his sister up and gave her a bear hug, bouncing her up and down in his arms the way he used to when she was a baby.

She nuzzled into his shoulder and whispered, "I was just coming to wake you for breakfast. Daddy made pancakes!"

Archie breathed a sigh of relief at the news his dad hadn't relapsed. The last thing he needed was to be marooned at home when Georgia needed him.

"That sounds awesome! I bet you can't wait to eat them, huh?" he felt Katie nod her head next to his. "Well, let's get to it then."

Archie galloped down the stairs with Katie in his arms, leaving a trail of giggles behind them. When they arrived at the kitchen, their dad had just finished plating up and was smiling at them both.

"Pancake anyone?"

On each plate sat a neat stack of homemade pancakes covered in maple syrup. Archie couldn't shun his dad's efforts, but he couldn't leave Georgia to face Crooked House alone either. He figured if he delayed Georgia by promising to meet her there, he'd be able to keep everyone happy. Plus, he'd have a far better chance of talking Georgia out of breaking in if they were face to face.

"Thanks dad, they look amazing. I just need to text Richard from school as I was going to meet up with him this morning if that's ok?"

He hated lying, but he couldn't tell his dad what he was really up to as he'd never let him out.

"Of course, Arch, you go have fun with your mates. That's what half-term is all about at your age." His dad was settling into his newfound role well, considering he'd been largely absent for the last ten months.

Archie joined them at the table and sent a quick message to Georgia.

```
Ok give me 45 mins and I'll be
there. Don't go in without
me! Xxx
```

He realized he'd sent her a capital kiss as it autocorrected and wondered if that would scare her off. He'd heard uppercase kisses had an entirely different meaning to lowercase ones. As he twisted his brain into even more knots, he felt his phone buzz in his hand and glanced down at her reply.

```
K, but don't leave me hanging!
Xxx
```

Archie beamed as he stuffed a forkful of fluffy pancake into his mouth.

Just a few days ago everything felt overwhelmingly bleak, and yet here he was eating pancakes with the people he loved and about to have a secret rendezvous with a gorgeous girl he'd just met.

He thought about Peter's message and figured he'd better reply to put his mind at ease.

Taking another forkful of breakfast, he typed.

Hey Peter,

It was great to speak to you yesterday and thanks again for showing an interest in my work. I found out who the girl was at Crooked House yesterday and it turns out she is Jonathan Ashfield's daughter.

I think she may be next in line to disappear, so I'm going to meet her there today and warn her off for good.

I promise when I'm done, I'll never go back there again.

Thought you should know in case you were worried.

Anyway, here is a poem I wrote recently. I've not shared my work before so if it's terrible then please go easy on me.

I originally wrote it about my dad, but I guess it's as much about me too.

Hope you like it...

My Darkness
by Archie Faulkner

There are no limits to the depths I'll dive
No shadow in which I will not hide
You see, I'm tired
Tired of the light
That blinding, binding, all consuming light
That others have and I would like
And so I stay here, safe in my darkness
Personal and private
Hiding in plain sight

As Archie hit send, he felt a warm sense of satisfaction. Somehow he'd managed to keep everyone happy, without any sacrifice of his own.

He paused for a moment to take in the room, watching Katie put pancakes away like she was posting letters; her face covered in syrup. He looked across at his dad and caught him looking right back at him. They gave each other a knowing nod and continued their morning feast.

Archie was no fool; he knew they weren't out of the woods yet, but this was a start and that's all any of them could ask for after all they had been through.

"Thanks dad, that was amazing!" Archie collected the empty plates and carried them to the sink.

"Leave that Arch, I'll do it. You go and catch up with Richard. Maybe when you get back we can all watch a movie together and I'll do some popcorn?"

"You're on. I'll text you when I'm on my way back, ok?" Archie kissed his sister on the top of her head and then threw an arm around his dad's shoulder on his way to the back door.

Something deep inside him didn't want to leave them in that almost perfect moment, but leave he did.

He couldn't keep Georgia waiting.

When he arrived at Crooked House, there was an eerie silence.

There were no birds or wildlife to be heard amongst the trees, and the wind that had battered him the entire ride there had now dwindled into nothing.

The sky was dark, heavy with thick grey clouds, and the smell of damp wood clogged Archie's lungs. It had all the hallmarks of a storm gathering.

The building itself looked like it had aged since his last visit, and as he approached, he noticed a series of large cracks, like giant claw marks, scattered around the front door frame.

A feeling of unease brewed in the pit of his stomach as he wandered the grounds in search of Georgia.

"Hello?"

His voice barely penetrated the dense air surrounding him; it was as if he'd stepped into a vacuum. A sharp crunch sounded behind him; a twig snapping underfoot.

Spinning around, he glimpsed the tail end of a shadow moving behind one of the trees in front of him.

"You're not funny, Georgia," he called, hoping to flush her out.

He checked his phone; still no signal, but there was one unread message.

```
Hey, got tired of waiting so
I'll meet u inside. I loosened
a board around the back so u
can squeeze in through that. C
u soon Xxx
```

Archie's mouth went dry and his colour drained as he read the message.

He took a step closer towards the tree where he'd seen the shadow.

"Hello? Who's there?" He eyed his bike to see how quickly he could reach it and figured he'd be better off on foot if things went sideways.

Thud!

Archie jumped out of his skin as the window behind him shook from within. He turned and through the grease and grime, he saw Georgia's nose pressed against the glass inside.

She smiled and beckoned him inside.

She looked every bit as gorgeous as she had the day before, and Archie doubled over with his hands on his knees in search of his composure.

"Come out here? It's not safe in there!" He nervously divided his attention between Georgia and the trees behind him. This was not how Archie saw the morning playing out at all.

"Come inside" she dug her heels in. "You need to see this place. I think I've found the files, too."

As Archie took a step closer to the window, he noticed movement in the background.

At first he thought it was a reflection, but when he twisted to look over his shoulder, there was nothing behind him but desolate trees. Turning back towards Georgia he noticed a shadow lurking behind her inside. It was large and moving towards her.

Before Archie had a chance to open his mouth and warn her, Georgia let out a bloodcurdling scream as the shadow dragged her away into the darkness of Crooked House.

"Georgia!" he bellowed, thumping the glass with his fist.

He rushed around to the rear of the house in search of a way in.

At the base of the back door, nailed to the frame, was a square panel of wood. Archie grabbed it with both hands and prized it away from the door, just enough until he could scramble through the gap on all fours. The panel snapped shut behind him and he found himself immersed in total darkness.

"Georgia!" he cried. "Where are you?"

Another scream came from down the hall and Archie sprinted blindly towards it.

As he reached the end of the hallway, he made out a wide-open space ahead of him. A further scream rang out to his right, so he set off in pursuit down another hallway. This one was even darker than the last, and there was no way Archie would make it any further without a torch.

He inched forward, one step at a time, with one hand outstretched ahead of him, whilst the other fumbled in his pocket for his phone.

"Archie! Please help me!" Georgia's desperate plea echoed down the corridor from up ahead.

Finally, Archie found the flashlight setting on his phone and directed it in front of him.

An icy shiver rippled through his body instantly as the brilliant white beam of light struck the door up ahead to reveal a brass number nine.

Another scream shook him from his daze, and he forced himself to march onward.

Just as Archie's hand clasped the door handle of room 9 his phone vibrated, shaking him to the core.

The message preview showed it was from Peter and it read.

```
Do not go anywhere until I get
there. Jonathan never had a
daughter…
```

Archie's blood ran cold, and he felt dizzy, as if was about to faint. He tightened his grip on the handle to steady himself. His brain was firing ten to the dozen as he tried to make sense of what he'd just read.

Before he could do anything, before his instincts told him to run as far away from Crooked House as his unsteady legs would carry him, the door to room 9 swung violently inward and dragged Archie a couple of steps inside. His legs threatened to buckle beneath him as he struggled to find his balance.

Georgia was leaning casually up against the wall furthest from the door. She had a wry smile on her face and wasn't in any danger at all.

"Welcome to room 9 Archie. We've been waiting for you."

Georgia's voice was different somehow. She sounded cold and almost robotic.

She pulled back the blonde bobbed wig she had been wearing and tossed it on the ground at Archie's feet. Her entire image changed in a heartbeat as she shook her long, wavy brunette hair loose from its confines and smiled at him, a wicked smile of triumph.

Archie had been a fool, blinded by her from the moment they'd met.

The door slammed shut behind him, and Archie turned to meet her accomplice.

A towering hulk of a man stepped out from the shadows. Dressed entirely in black, his chiselled face was ashen, and a shock of pure white hair stood on end atop his head. The behemoth's eyes were closed, and he took in a huge deep breath, sending his colossal chest up towards his chin.

Holding his breath in contemplation as if he was enjoying the aroma of a fine wine, he then let out a long, satisfying sigh and opened his eyes. Hypnotic, raven orbs glistened from the depths of his deep, sunken eye sockets. Devoid of any emotion, the monster sized up his prey and took a measured step forward.

Archie momentarily saw the light from his phone bounce off the knife the man-mountain was holding, but he couldn't react.

Paralyzed by fear, or some other strange enchantment, his body was rigid and unresponsive.

Georgia's laughter echoed around him as the bogeyman grabbed Archie by the throat, an inhuman, vice-like grip which lifted him clean off the ground.

He felt the knife the first time.

It was cold and sharp as it entered his stomach, but with each new thrust he felt less and less.

The warm tears that streamed down his face, the metallic river of blood rising in his mouth, faded into nothingness as Archie hung lifeless, like a piñata in the hands of a sweet-crazed child.

Blow upon blow showered the floor with crimson candy that glimmered under the dim light of his discarded phone.

Archie's relatively brief life rushed past him like a distant dream; trips to the park with his dad; his first bike; the birth of Katie and the giggles she filled his home with; then finally his mum, still finding the strength to smile at him from her hospital bed.

A sudden rush of panic washed over him, a desperate yearning to see them all one last time, which sent his heart racing to its final beat and Archie Faulkner was no more.

50

Peter dragged his foot over the dirt, erasing the bleak diagram he'd drawn for everyone.

"There is more to this place than just the monsters lurking in its halls, I'm afraid. There are others...people... hiding in plain sight. Dangerous people who will stop at nothing to see the prophecy fulfilled. I was too late for Archie, but this time, it will be different. It must be..."

"Too late...wait, that's the message in room 9. Is Archie the boy under the bed?" Izzy blurted the second she'd made the connection.

Peter solemnly nodded and closed his eyes again.

"Ah, you found Helen's files...that's very smart of you all. Crooked House had a helper that day...a girl. I don't know who she was, but I'm convinced she lured Archie into this place and by the time I arrived... he was gone."

"The blood was everywhere in that room. What happened?" JJ was quick to ask what everyone else was thinking.

"I'll never know. When I arrived here that day, Archie was already gone. The room was spotless and there was no sign of any foul play. The image you've all seen...the one with the blood... that was captured a couple of months later. Helen sent it to me, along with the access codes to the live camera feeds. That was the last time I heard from her before she disappeared, and the room has been dormant ever since. In fact, the entire house had been dormant until yesterday."

"So how come we saw another me in room 6? Was that a ghost?" Zach had been desperate to ask since he'd arrived.

"None of the occupants of Crooked House are ghosts, well, not in the traditional sense at least. They are more like echoes or ripples in time. Time doesn't always play by the rules here, as you've seen in those files. My working theory is that each echo possesses something unique which the shadow creatures need in order to fulfil their prophecy. Whether it's their soul, or their specific frequency; I don't quite know, yet. However, the echoes are definitely not chosen at random, so there must be some form of selection criteria; otherwise this would have all been over a long time ago. The little evidence I have suggests the closer they get to their intended victim, the more likely we are to see a projection of them pop up inside the house. We saw it with Jessica, and that's also why you showed up Zach. They have been waiting for you, which means we are close to the end. During my research, I discovered that this place is supposedly built on a concentration of dark energy, so it acts as the bridge between our world and what is known as the shadow realm. It's why they have so much power here. I'm just glad I found you in time..."

"But you said each universe is fixed?" Izzy challenged.

"Ah, yes, that's true. But I have another hypothesis, if we somehow got ahead of fate and uncovered what lies ahead, then we could potentially alter things... or at the very least, challenge them. That's why I've brought you all here today. I believe we are at that juncture…"

Clap…clap….clap…

The slow cynical sound stopped everyone in their tracks. They all looked at each other and then searched for the source of the interruption. There, in the shadow of the porch, stood one of the creatures and it was mocking them all.

"What a delightful story, Peter."

Its voice was more human than the other monsters they had encountered. Although there was still a slight clunkiness to it, it sounded smart. Sarcastic.

"You cannot stop us. The end is already written, and it's upon you."

The group immediately put themselves between the creature and Zach, shielding him from its gaze.

"It was foolish to come here."

"You have no power here!" Peter bellowed with authority, gesturing towards the clear blue-sky and winter sunshine.

"You underestimate us." The chilling reply echoed from the building's empty hallway.

"You are on our soil now." Its second sentence came from outside the house this time.

Six hearts all skipped a beat in unison as their eyes darted around in search of the source.

The creature was no longer on the porch and was now standing behind Zach under the shade of a large oak tree. Its arms were around him like a proud parent!

Zach trembled as he looked down at the spindly fingers draped over his shoulders. He was paralyzed with fear by the creature's long, crooked nails, which looked as if they could slice through steel.

Glancing up, he realized the distance between him and the group was too great for anyone to intervene. Besides, one false move and he might literally lose his head.

"Let him go!" snapped Kane. He felt sick to his stomach and powerless.

They had played right into the creature's lethal hands.

Peter swiftly guided the children behind him while raising his arms to make himself as wide a barrier as possible.

"It doesn't have to be this way," he begged, his voice breaking under the weight of regret that was now threatening to bury him where he stood. A cold sweat had broken out on the back of his neck and a feeling of utter dread was congealing in the pit of his stomach.

"It's already this way," the creature spat back in demented glee, *"It's always been this way, you fool!"*

And with the deftest of motions, the monster put his deadly nails to work, slicing the boy's throat.

Zach's blood escaped with a trickle at first, slowly seeping into the collar of his sweater.

The crimson trickle soon became a stream, as his broken heart laboured frantically, pumping his life out onto the grass for all to see.

Raising his head in confusion, Zach ceased shuddering.

He felt calm. Still.

A serene weightlessness washed over him as if he was floating on a cloud of numbness and indifference.

His eyes opened; black as night and were greeted by the desperate screams of all those he cared about.

Several decibels higher than anyone, he could hear his brother crying uncontrollably until it all faded into silence and everything went dark. It was over.

Zach was gone.

51

"Noooooooooo!" Kane leapt forward in rage, swinging his tennis racket at the head of the creature holding the body of his pale, blood-soaked baby brother.

They both evaporated in a dark mist, leaving the gnarled tree trunk to shoulder the brunt of Kane's fury. The powerful blow stung his palms when the rocklike tree refused to budge, but Kane didn't flinch.

He had just lost everything.

Before anyone else had a chance to react, the surrounding air whipped up into a gale, forcing them to shield their eyes from dried leaves and debris as it began pecking at them like ravenous birds.

Peter's confidence in the sun's protection quickly evaporated as the ground beneath them started to tremble and the sky turned a deep red. The wounded sun bled out into the crisp blue sky, turning it a burnt amber, as dark purple clouds gathered like vultures circling their prey. The once towering, sturdy oak that Kane had struck moments ago began to wither and die in front of them, as if the life was being sucked out of it from its roots.

Dazed and bewildered, Peter continued to do his best to shield them all from the vicious elements that were now reaping havoc around them. He ushered the remaining children to the clearing in front of Crooked House as an almighty thunderclap rang out above them, shattering all its windows. The noise was deafening, shaking them all to their core, while showering them in tiny fragments of broken glass that nicked and scratched like a swarm of angry wasps.

Izzy tumbled to her knees in the bedlam. As she fumbled around trying to find her glasses, her hand landed on something smooth and waxy to the touch. She looked up, expecting to see Peter, but instead found herself under the towering shadow of a monster.

His eyes were beyond black, far darker than any of the creatures they had seen. There was no sign of a sparkle within them. He looked stone-cold and completely soulless. The storm didn't seem to affect him at all, as he stood strong and unmoved whilst trees bent and buckled around him.

Bending down, he yanked Izzy up by her mousy brown ponytail until she no longer felt the ground beneath her.

Face to face, she recognized the shock of white hair blowing wildly in the wind and that's when she noticed the hunter's knife clenched in his hand.

"Noooo! Please! Help me...somebody..." Kicking and screaming, she searched desperately for her friends, but she had been separated in the confusion.

Dangling helplessly, Izzy realized no-one was there to save her from the boogeyman in room 4, and any fight she had left gave way to tears of surrender.

The relentless storm drowned out her final cries as The Demon of Cold Christmas gleefully hacked and slashed at Izzy until her body fell limp and her soul was lost.

"Izzy!!" JJ yelled as he watched the killer toss her body to the ground, but the air swallowed his voice before it had a chance to sound.

Breaking free from the group, he charged toward the sinister figure, battling the wind as best he could; determined to make him pay for what he'd just done.

The ground shook more intensely as he got closer, and JJ struggled to keep his balance. A vast crack emerged, pelting everyone with dirt and debris as it raced across the lifeless grass. JJ crashed to the ground as the clearing violently split in two.

Catching his breath, he looked up to find the dark figure was now within touching distance. He jumped to his feet and swung his bat with every bit of strength he had left. Hampered by the wind, he connected with the man's large open hand who caught it effortlessly. He snatched the weapon away as if JJ was a newborn baby waving a rattle.

His black, callous eyes stared through the teenager in front of him, unflapped by the attack, and he calmly grabbed JJ by the scruff of his jumper.

Squirming and pounding at the stone-cold hand at his throat, JJ tried to break free, but it was like punching granite. He was hoisted into the air with supernatural ease.

Face to face with the monster, JJ's blood drained from his face as he dangled precariously over the chasm that had now opened in the ground behind them.

Looking down, all he could see was darkness, as if he was being held over a bottomless pit. JJ stopped thumping the hand that gripped him and tried desperately to hold on, but he wasn't strong enough. Trying to defend against the bloodstained knife being thrust at him was equally futile.

Each relentless blow connected with such savage force, the blade passed all the way through JJ's body, breaking out through his back and glistening beneath the angry sun. A waterfall of blood ensued, gushing from his mouth and choking him as it covered the killer's hand. His bloodlust quenched, the boogeyman calmly discarded JJ's lifeless body like a rubbish bag and watched him disappear into the depths of the earth.

"Noooooooo!" Kane cried in despair as he saw his best friend plummet to his death.

"I'll fucking kill you for this!" he screamed at the hulking shadow dripping with blood, but the chasm between them was now so vast he was too far away to exact any revenge.

Beside himself with a rage and sorrow that tangled him in knots, his legs shook beneath him as he teetered on a knife's edge with nowhere to go.

He glanced around to find Peter had lost whatever remained of his composure, looking like he was on the verge of his own private breakdown.

Furrowing his brow, he darted his eyes from left to right, searching for a plan.

It was over.

He had lost everything; just like his brother's ghost had warned them.

Kane dropped to his knees. Coming down from his adrenalin rush, his fighting spirit deserted him.

What was the point, anyway?

The world they knew and loved was on the brink of destruction, and it was all his stupid fault. As he knelt, dejected and in pieces, he didn't notice the enormous creature rising from the darkness behind him.

Long, bony fingers danced like spider legs along the edge of the crater, looking for something to grip onto.

Meridia looked on in horror as a giant hooded figure pulled itself out of the ground.

It stood upright on the brink of the hole that had swallowed JJ and cast a malign shadow over the three remaining survivors. This monster was at least twice the size of the one they had banished with sunlight.

Long, dark shadowy robes ebbed and flowed gracefully with the wind, as if the creature was conducting the storm that now battered the land.

This was death itself.

Peter snapped out of his mental collapse and raced toward Kane, who was oblivious; consumed by his grief.

Death's robes lashed out like a cluster of tentacles, stopping Peter in his tracks.

Viciously hoisted into the air, Peter struggled and winced in pain as the robes tightened around his body like a deadly slap-band, until he was completely mummified.

Meridia watched on in terror as Peter convulsed from within his dark cocoon and then fell limp.

The robe unfolded, and all that was left of poor Peter was ash.

His tiny grey particles whooshed and whirled in the wind before dispersing into the murderous sky.

Kane just knelt there, accepting of his fate.

So much pain and bloodshed had scorched his eyes, he couldn't find the resolve to get back to his feet.

He looked up at Death looming over him and shook his head in resignation.

Once again, the robes lashed out, ensnaring their next victim. There was no struggle this time.

As the deadly fabric worked its way up to Kane's grief-stricken face, he locked eyes with Meridia and mouthed the words, *'I'm sorry'*.

His dust blew upwards in the wind, spiralling in the air as if in search of his lost friends.

Meridia felt the warmth of her tears as they streamed down her cheeks, stunned and in shock, as she sat on the desolate ground outside Crooked House, unable to comprehend the horrors that had unfolded.

The hooded reaper was still, like the eye of a storm surrounded by destruction and carnage. It raised its head in Meridia's direction and locked eyes with her.

There, beneath its cloak, Meridia came face to face with the true horror of Crooked House.

The flesh of its victims wrapped every inch of the monsters' cadaverous skull, resembling a trophy mask. As it drew closer, Meridia saw Peter, Kane, Izzy, Zach and JJ all writhing in torturous agony, clinging onto its twisted face, condemned to eternal torment.

Eyes ablaze with hatred, the hideous beast let out an unearthly, ghastly scream and burst towards her at supernatural speed, engulfing her in darkness.

52

Merida felt weightless in the dark, like a feather blowing gently in the breeze. She was calm, happy even, which was odd given what she'd just witnessed.

None of that mattered anymore.

Nothing did.

For the first time in her life, she was completely free and at ease, which was ironic given she'd just died.

A vague colour snaked into her awareness; the way light does behind closed eyes. It was difficult to discern at first, largely because she no long had any eyes. At least, not that she could feel. In fact, she couldn't feel anything. Not in any traditional, physical way. But somehow, she sensed the colour, and it was beautiful.

Hypnotic.

Hues of blue twisted and turned into a purple haze, as if someone was stirring two pots of paint inside her mind.

In the distant depths of her consciousness, she noticed the rhythmic sound of a heartbeat.

The kaleidoscope of colour attached itself to the noise as it grew louder, and they both danced together. It was an elegant dance that was as dazzling as it was mesmerizing, and all Meridia wanted to do was to stay, but something began pulling her away. She tried to focus on the waltzing colours, but the more she concentrated, the more elusive they became.

Gradually they faded back into the darkness from where they came, and she was alone again, tumbling through the air. The further she fell, the heavier she became, until finally she landed with the force of a cannon ball.

The surrounding air had grown thick like tar, drowning her as she struggled to move. She wriggled and writhed, sinking all the more; deeper and deeper, until she fell freely again, as if she'd been caught in a floating river of glue.

Somewhere in the distance, she heard voices, like the remnants of a dream. A conversation drifted into her awareness as if she was slowly waking from a deep sleep.

Her senses came flooding back as she softly touched down on the ground. A gentle, cool breeze tickled her cheeks and Meridia tentatively opened her eyes.

53

"Hey, it's ok Zach," Peter continued "I've found you first. I think we can stop them this time."

"What do you mean 'this time'?" Kane probed.

"The shadow people are limited to the souls they must take. I had a chance to stop them before, but I got there too late. I blew it..." Peter hung his head and stared solemnly at the circles in the dirt.

"Archie?" Meridia declared without thinking. She looked up to see Peter closing his eyes and nodding slowly.

"Wait! How do you know about Archie? What's going on?" Peter trailed off.

A slow clapping sound broke out from somewhere to Meridia's left. She turned right and yanked Zach out from under the shade of an old oak into the sunlight.

"What was that for?" Zach complained with a start.

Before she could explain, the shadowy creature appeared in the space Zach had vacated. For a moment it looked just as confused as Zach, the way parents sometimes enter a room only to forget what they went in there for. It glared at Meridia as she let go of Zach's arm, and a deep frown formed like a thunderstorm brewing above its glistening eyes.

"*A seer!*" it hissed in frustration. "*This changes nothing! You are nothing. The Rising has begun! There is nothing you can do to stop us.*"

Kane wasn't sure what had just happened.

Nobody was.

He watched the twisted silhouette protesting under the shade of the oak tree and thought about the wicked witch in The Wizard of Oz. He wondered what would happen if he threw a bucket of water over it...The monster was directing all its anger at Meridia, like she'd stolen its lunch money. He was definitely missing something.

"It's over! You've lost!" Meridia countered. Her steely blue eyes shimmered in defiance under the safety of the sun's rays.

The group watched in stunned silence as Meridia turned her back on the beast.

"You're nothing," she said brazenly. Her hands were shaking now, but she stood her ground and addressed the group. "We need to get as far away from this place as possible and never come back. They've been feeding on our fear since we got here. They're nothing! Trust me...They have no power over us...they're nothing but shadows..."

The monster exploded in a fit of rage.

"*You dare dismiss me, child?!*" a foul wind bellowed out of the creature's cavernous mouth, exposing row upon row of razor-sharp teeth. Overcome with rage, its body rattled like a volcano threatening to violently erupt, while its vague, shadowy features sharpened and contorted with anger.

Meridia held her nerve and continued to ignore the creature as it stewed in its own juices under the shade of the oak tree. Fluorescent, shining black orbs of hate burned a hole in her back as she gestured for her friends to depart.

The beast loomed above her now; its bony claws of death reaching high into the air, ready to come down like a hammer and shred the girl beneath. The tension became unbearable as Kane and JJ tightened their grip on their weapons in readiness, but Meridia remained unflustered. If she was bluffing, she was doing a remarkable job.

"C'mon guys, we're done here. It's over...we've won. Just make sure you stay in the light and there's nothing this pathetic creature can do to harm you. Crooked House can rot in hell, and all its monsters can rot with it. Find another world to end." The longer they were alive, the more Meridia's confidence grew. Her tone took on one of a veteran fighter, who had the measure of their opponent.

The group almost heard the last strand of the creature's restraint snap just before it swooped down and lunged at them all in frustration.

A warm, dark mist that smelled like burnt matches blew across the back of Meridia, dissolving into the air in front of her as light triumphed over darkness.

One last venomous scream of horror rang out in the clearing. It echoed amongst the trees, chasing birds away from their homes, before fading into nothing, just as the creature had.

Meridia took a deep breath and steadied her shredded nerves.

"Let's go home."

54

Confused, and befuddled the group all left the grounds of Crooked House at Meridia's insistence and made their way to the park. She didn't even know where to begin when they arrived. Silent and withdrawn the entire journey back, Peter had taken it upon himself to fill the awkward silence with paranormal anecdotes from his travels around the world. Despite the daunting circumstances, he'd somehow raised almost everyone's spirits, convincing them they could conquer the world, or at least save it. Meridia however, was less convinced.

Eyes firmly locked to the ground as she walked, the terrors she had seen weighed heavy on her. By the time they all arrived at the park gates she had decided against sharing everything she had witnessed, instead offering a vague outline of the tragic outcome. She didn't want to burden anyone with the horror of it all. Besides, she still didn't fully understand what was happening to her.

'*What was a seer, anyway?*' She worried about what the others might think. That she would be labelled a freak, or crazy, like her father! Once she had finished telling her abridged story, everyone huddled around Meridia in support. They all knew she was holding something back, but nobody pressed.

"So, what do we do now?" Zach asked.

"I made a terrible mistake bringing you all here," Peter began, "One that it seems I was doomed to make. We got lucky today, thanks to you, my dear. Like it or not, you may be the key to saving our world. We still have a long way to go however. Make no mistake, we won the battle today, but the invisible war rages on and the balance is still tipped in their favour. We are living in times of war and corruption, unprecedented food shortages and all under the constant threat from the next pandemic. This is all their work, and they are getting stronger with or without Zach. This is so much bigger than Crooked House, I'm convinced of it. The world isn't losing its way or going mad. It is being driven to the brink of self-destruction by them. So Zach, in answer to your question; we regroup. We come back stronger, more informed, and we do everything we can to turn this war around. After all, we find ourselves in a brand-new world today, and that means anything is possible."

Peter's battle cry was inspiring, yet Meridia's eyes stayed glued to the grass at her feet. Its gentle swaying in the breeze was mildly soothing and gave her something to focus on. She wasn't coming out of her shell anytime soon, despite the newfound buoyance in the group. She pictured them all; her best friends that were her world and wondered if they ever would tip the scales back in their favour. She was desperate to believe they could, but next to her, a stark reminder showed they were still headed for failure.

An all-too-familiar angel of death had been by her side the entire walk back from Crooked House and now stood loyally at her shoulder. Invisible to her friends, she had avoided his gaze the entire journey, ignoring his incessant whispering.

Pretending to herself he wasn't there.

But he was so close now she could feel his icy breath on her cheek.

She couldn't ignore him anymore.

Eyes closed, she searched within herself for whatever courage she had left and surrendered to his will.

He reached up and pulled his dirty blue hoodie down to reveal those unearthly glistening eyes. Black tears stained his pale, lifeless cheeks as he solemnly shook his head.

"It wasn't enough Meridia... They're all coming for you now..."

EPILOGUE
YEARS LATER

The decaying corrugated iron of the old-shed roof rattled under the relentless onslaught of acid rain. No matter how much the skies wept these days, it was never enough to resurrect the long-lost sun from its gloomy grave.

The stench of death hung heavily in the sodden air, seeping its way in under the barricaded door and clogging Meridia's lungs as she waited silently for the downpour to pass. She now spent most of her evenings this way, unable to distinguish between night and day anymore.

Cold Christmas was nothing more than a murky graveyard, steeped in tragedy and horror. Its streets were desolate, awash with the blood of so many innocents. Ignorant spectators of a dark, cancerous war that now rampaged from town to town, scorching the earth in its wake.

Crooked House had just been the tip of a deadly iceberg. An atomic bomb whose timer had been started long ago by another player in the game, hiding in plain sight. Cold Christmas had been the real threat all along. Its many secrets protected by The Children of the Shadows.

Pulling the strings from the very beginning as they wove their intricate web of manipulation and terror. A web that ensnared JJ all those years ago, sowing a seed in his mind that would change their lives forever. Seduced by the thrill of fame and adventure, five friends had foolishly entered a haunted hotel in search of scares.

Those days were nothing more than a distant dream now.

A nostalgic movie that Meridia had once loved, but would never see again.

The years that followed were all lost to a life on the run, hiding in the very shadows she had been so fearful of. She felt Izzy's hand rest on hers.

"The fire's ready now. Come and warm up." Meridia searched around for the gnarled branch by her side and drove it into the ground as she rose to her feet.

"The blind seer...Ha!" the monster's spiteful words echoed in her mind every time she gripped the rough bark in her palm.

Once on her feet, Izzy cradled Meridia and ushered her to the modest fire in the corner. The last battle took more than her eyes. They had suffered heavy casualties at the hands of the sinister cult, including JJ.

Oh, how she longed to be twelve again, and back in Zach's garden that bright winter's morning. The five of them, untainted by the evil of Cold Christmas and its many monsters.

Nobody even knew where Zach was anymore. Their plan to keep him moving had indeed kept him alive and out of the creature's clutches, but at what cost?

As the beating rain continued to overload her remaining senses, Meridia wondered if this war-torn world was still worth fighting for.

Izzy guided her to the blanket next to the fire, and she knelt, listening to its soothing crackle, the warmth tickling her cheeks. She tried to clear her troubled mind, but all she could think of was Zach, out there in the wilderness they'd once called home.

Reaching into her pocket, she pulled out the Lego keyring he had given her before he'd left.

"So you can always find me," he'd told her.

She fondly caressed the plastic figure in her hand, tracing each contour with her thumb as she brought him into focus with the only eye she had left; the gift she never wanted. Meridia found his spiritual signature quickly, wading in loneliness and sorrow, as it often was. He was on the move again and she felt panic simmering deep within him. This had been a close call. They were getting smarter.

Since the government had fallen, it was difficult to travel far, not to mention dangerous. Survivors and looters drifted from town to town looking for shelter, ransacking supplies. Some were friendly, whilst others travelled in packs and were less so.

Civil war swept the country, leaving behind lawless streets and driving a final nail in the coffin of an already fragile society. Every town left for dead, needing to fend for itself as they fought over diminishing resources. This bleak landscape multiplied the number of threats Zach encountered on his travels and was the reason Meridia and Izzy still found themselves marooned in Cold Christmas.

The tiny resistance they had mobilized couldn't afford to lose both its prized assets in one attack. The creatures had played a cunning game. A game that was reaching its conclusion. Still, their best hope rested firmly on the shoulders of Peter and Kane, if they ever made it back.

Overwhelmed by his plight, Meridia turned her focus

away from Zach and dipped her attention in the river of time, but the future remained unchanged.

Perhaps the game was rigged after all?

Was another stay of execution the best they could hope for?

Hope was such a loaded word these days.

The very thought of it stung, provoking a deep-rooted resentment for everything she had endured.

Oh, to be twelve again.

Meridia wondered if it would be such a bad thing to concede. To rest her weary body and let go. Given everything they had already lost, would it offer sweet release from the endless suffering and torment? Deep down she knew she had no choice but to keep going.

The day of reckoning was almost upon them now, and one way or another the war would soon be over.

AUTHOR'S NOTE

Thank you for reading *The Rising*, book one of the *Crooked Tales Series*. Although some of the places described in this book are based on real locations, the stories told within are a complete work of fiction.

When I set out to write *The Rising*, I wanted to create something epic that captured all the elements of horror I enjoyed so much as a kid. Before I knew it, I had a series of five books on my hands: each one a love letter to a different sub-genre, so I hope you enjoy the ride. With any luck you'll discover a group of friends along the way that you can laugh, jump, and cry with, but ultimately relate to and root for as you join them on their journey into darkness.

This book also contains its fair share of macabre Easter Eggs, so good luck finding them all, and I look forward to seeing you again for the next instalment.

Acknowledgments

I'd like to thank Raymond, and everyone at *Wicked Ink Publishing* for believing in a first-time author and helping me fulfil a lifelong dream. You have made this journey an absolute joy from start to finish. Thank you for seeing the potential in my ideas and encouraging me to think bigger… and darker.

I'd like to thank my wife, Nikki, for being my rock throughout and supporting me on this brand-new adventure. Not only have you kept a close eye on my marbles whenever I was in danger of losing them, but you've always come up clutch whenever I've needed a kickass character name.

I'd like to thank my son, Harry, for being my biggest fan and for always believing in me no matter what.

To my best friend, Dene, you have been a constant source of encouragement that extends way beyond this book. You have helped me in more ways than you know.

I'd also like to thank Chivonne, for patiently listening to the early ramblings of a writer still trying to find his voice, and all my online advocates who have been cheering me on since I started.

Lastly, I'd like to thank the true masters of horror who shaped my nightmares as a child, Stephen King, Clive Barker, John Carpenter, and Dean Koontz. The ripple effect you created in this genre lit a fire in my imagination as a teenager and has kept me gripped ever since.

ABOUT THE AUTHOR

© Chris Harrison

Chris Harrison, born in North London, is not just a writer, producer, and author of the *Crooked Tales Series*; he's a storyteller on a mission. Graduating from Middlesex University with a degree in Film, Chris turned his fascination with the art of storytelling into a lifelong exploration of literary and cinematic horror. Having previously written for film and education, he's now dedicated to realizing a dream—crafting immersive worlds filled with spine-tingling terror for a young adult audience.

Chris's creations fuse classic supernatural themes with contemporary urban mythology, re-imagining our deepest fears for a new generation of horror enthusiasts.

www.chris-harrison.com

- instagram.com/chrisharrison1975
- threads.net/@chrisharrison1975
- tiktok.com/@chris.harrison75
- x.com/CHarrison22975

www.ingramcontent.com/pod-product-compliance
Ingram Content Group UK Ltd.
Pitfield, Milton Keynes, MK11 3LW, UK
UKHW010731160825
461893UK00001B/6